SET IN THE 80S AND 90S, A YOUNG WOMAN SEARCHES FOR TRUE LOVE AMID A SEA OF TOADS. FROM THE HIGH DRAMA OF TEEN ROMANCE TO THE AWKWARD INFANCY OF ONLINE DATING, HER SOULMATE MAY BE WAITING WHERE SHE LEAST EXPECTS IT.

.

"*Kissing Toads* is a page turning and charming literary treasure. Danissa Wilson masterfully brings the reader through Annie's search for love, as she learns lifelong lessons from many toads along the way. Themes of love, tragedy, and resilience are brilliantly weaved throughout the novel leaving the reader filled with confidence that true love does exist and that kissing a few toads on our path to self-discovery helps to reveal the strength within each of us, to recognize our own self-worth, and to appreciate the gifts already in front of us we couldn't have otherwise seen." ***—Danielle Augustin, JD, MA—Anaheim Hills, CA***

"Despite the specificity of the time period and the unique challenges that era presents, *Kissing Toads* is a generational story that dives freely into matters of the heart and mind. Whether it be through shallow waters or the deepest of oceans, Danissa Wilson skillfully uses humor to guide us through the often-painful universal realities of life, rendering them into a beautiful portrait of self-discovery." — ***Dakota Gorman, Writer/Director— NYC***

"Danissa Wilson's *Kissing Toads* is a beautiful coming-of-age story with themes of love, friendship, and perseverance. From beautiful and relatable character development to witty banter and finding love in all the wrong places, readers won't be able to put Wilson's debut novel down. *Kissing Toads* will leave you laughing, crying, and reminding you that love lies where you least expect it."—***Taylor Littlejohn— Newport Beach, CA***

"*Kissing Toads* is a must-read for anyone who appreciates poignant storytelling and relatable characters. Wilson skillfully navigates themes of love, friendship, and self-discovery with nuance and authenticity. *Kissing Toads* carries a resonance akin to the impactful narratives of Judy Blume that shaped a generation. Annie's quest for connection is articulated in a voice that underscores the intuitive recognition and transformative power of love. Full of humor, relatability, and heartfelt moments, Wilson proves herself to be a formidable new talent in the literary world, poised to make a lasting impact for years to come."—***Jenni L. McCullum MFT, PCC—New Mexico***

"Wilson's inaugural novel *Kissing Toads* is a compelling depiction of the human condition. We follow Annie's journey of life through the lens of comedy and tragedy in the pursuit of love, independence, and happiness. Despite Annie getting knocked down multiple times, we witness the true strength of humanity's core: perseverance and hope."—***J.T. McLean – Alta Loma, CA***

"*Kissing Toads* is uniquely hilarious and heartfelt, a modern love story of self-discovery infused with Gen X nostalgia. Wilson's smart and observant writing inspires both laughter and tears as we root for Annie to find her true love."—***Kristine Nikkhoo, MA — Fullerton, CA***

A feminist tale at heart, Kissing Toads *is a fictitious memoir that tells the story of a now 50-something-year-old woman named Annie who takes the reader on her decades-long quest to find her "Prince Charming." Believing that if she kisses enough toads, she will eventually find her prince, Annie has one goal as a budding young woman: fetch herself a man. Set in the late 1970s through the mid-1990s, the reader follows Annie throughout young adulthood as she searches for her soulmate amid the backdrop of misogyny, a loving but overbearing mother, and gender and societal expectations. Sometimes cheeky, sometimes heartbreaking,* Kissing Toads *explores Annie's messy yet authentic misadventures in dating. But just when you think you've reached the happily-ever-after, brace yourself for an exhilarating plot twist.* Kissing Toads *is not just another coming-of-age tale; it's a celebration of self-discovery, liberation, and the courage to write your own fairy tale.*

KISSING TOADS

Danissa Wilson

Moonshine Cove Publishing, LLC

Bowling Green, Virginia U.S.A.

Moonshine Cove Edition September 2024

ISBN: 9781952439865

Library of Congress LCCN: 2024916474

Front cover illustration courtesy of Susan Zeng; back cover design and interior design by Moonshine Cove staff.

For my prince, Matt, and my loves:

Johnny, Jimmy, and Brady.

Thank you for being my everything.

About the Author

Initially inspired by one of her girlfriends who, fresh off a divorce, dove headfirst into the online dating scene (with disastrous results), DANISSA WILSON wrote this novel with the desire to explore the complexities of dating and finding one's sexual identity in the late 20th century. A Southern California native, Wilson holds a BA and MA in English as well as a doctorate in education. She taught creative writing, literature, and composition at the college level for more than a decade and has been working as a college library dean since 2014. When not writing, Wilson enjoys reading novels, stargazing, and spending time with her devoted partner, her three fun-loving children, and her three loyal pups. *Kissing Toads* is her first novel.

Website:

http://www.kissingtoadsnovel.com

Acknowledgment

I have immeasurable gratitude for many incredible women who helped me along my writing journey: Alison, who inspired me to write this novel in the first place; Danielle, who showed me that writing a book is an attainable goal; Kristine, who read my manuscript before anyone else and gave me invaluable feedback; Jenni, who gave me the cover idea as well as the confidence to keep going; Susan, who brought the cover to life; and Jill, who continues to be my guiding light, always.

Introduction

My name is Annie. At least, that's what I prefer to be called. My "real," full, name is Annabelle. *Annabelle*. Lord, what an insufferable name. Get this: my mom named me after one of her favorite pet dogs, a Golden Retriever by the name of Liberty's Lady Annabelle. Yeah, that was the dog's actual, legal, *pedigreed*, name. My mother claimed that the pup was the great-granddog (is that even a real thing?) of our 38th President of the United States, Gerald Ford. However, this "fact" cannot be verified. Hmph. How convenient.

But ah, a presidential pup, a POUTS heir, a *regal* dog, she would remind me. She couldn't have been more proud to own this noble canine. However, she was also regularly annoyed that I didn't appreciate my name more.

"How is it, Annabelle, that you are not *thrilled* to bear the name of this very important being?" my mother would demand in exasperation.

Gee mom, I would think to myself, *I wonder why. Being the namesake of the family pooch? Does it get more humiliating than that?*

Indeed, it was great fun at social gatherings as a child. Mom would hunt down anyone who would listen.

"Hello, Margaret! So nice to see you. Have you met my daughter, Annabelle? She's named after the descendent of American royalty, you know!" She would beam with pride as she spoke.

Don't ask, Margaret. Please, for God's sake, don't ask, I would silently pray.

And so it went. I was named after my mom's first love: her canine companion Annabelle. Well, to be honest, Annabelle was just one of her faithful "fur-babies." There was also Starbelle, Cooper and Toby. Starbelle and Cooper were actual puppies of Annabelle. So, they were also, by default, heir to the Ford legacy. However, make no mistake. It was Toby (and not one of the Ford offspring) that was the most revered dog of the house. My mother had an oil-painting portrait of Toby hanging in her bedroom. *A goddamn portrait*! Thank the Lord that masterpiece was not suspended in the living room. I'd have to suffer the painful reminder of my place in the family at more regular intervals. I could just imagine the humiliation I would suffer when I entertained my high school friends at home.

"Welcome to my house!" I would say, as I led them in the front door, through the small entryway, into our modest but comfortable living room. "May I offer you a cold beverage?"

"Lovely home," they'd exclaim. "Do you have any Tab? As you can imagine, I am watching my figure." Then, as if startled by the absurdity of it, they would remark: "Oh! Is that an oil on canvas portrait of your family's recently-deceased canine there on your living room wall?"

Ok, I am not sure why I visualized these teenaged friends of mine speaking like middle-aged divorcees, but the point stands. I would be mortified.

Much to the surprise and chagrin of my father and me, after Toby passed (in the back corner of our dining room, at the ripe old age of 13), my mother commissioned a portrait of him, and she hung that magnum opus above her bed. His slate black collar gently hung from the corner of that very portrait, golden engraved nametag precariously dangling from the bottom. This homage became a physical reminder of the loss that she suffered, a loss that she rarely let us forget. Words like *soulmate* and *kindred spirit* crossed her lips when referring to Toby.

It's not that I held any ill-will toward the pooch. I absolutely did not. I loved Toby as much as any little girl could love a dog. As I was the only child in the family, Toby was my playmate and my de facto brother. He kept the monsters under my bed at bay, and he kept me company on long family road trips across country. He suffered my attempts at riding him like a pony (poor dog—I am not sure how I didn't break his back), and he put up with me brushing his hair and attempting to put colorful ribbons in it. But for all the care and affection I shelled out to that dog, it paled in comparison to the kind of deep and reverent love that my mother felt for him.

To say my mother was an "animal lover" would be a gross understatement. She was an animal fanatic... dare I say *maniac*. She was the type of animal lunatic who refused to use a can of Raid to vanquish an ant infestation. Instead, she would seek to lure the tiny creatures out of the house with a celery stick dipped in honey. Unbeknownst to her, my father and I would fry the shit out of them with the poison when she wasn't around. We would later applaud her success in ushering the ants out to the greener pastures of our backyard. Yes, I realize we only served to perpetuate the situation. But, nah, we didn't have the heart to tell her.

In addition to dog-rearing, she also loved gardening. She took great pride in the bounty that was produced in her well-tended and manicured fruit and vegetable garden that she kept afloat on the side yard of our house. She grew tomatoes, bell peppers, cucumbers, strawberries, and several varieties of herbs and spices. When she would find garden snails on one of her plants, she would get upset, but she wouldn't just smash them, or put poison down, or throw them away in the garbage can like a "ruthless savage" (her words). Instead, she would double bag them in Ziplocks and deep freeze them in the standing freezer in the garage. According to her, this was the most humane way to dispose of the creatures.

"When flash frozen like this, Annabelle," she would instruct me in earnest, "the little buggers feel no pain."

My dad about shit a brick the first time he reached into the standing freezer to retrieve a piece of salmon from his latest fishing expedition only to find a baggie of dead snails. “Jesus Christ, honey!” I would hear him holler from the garage, “Are we eating escargot now, or do we need to have a conversation…?”

Yeah, so that was the way she treated insects. Imagine the life she gave to her beloved canines. It was lavish to say the least. My father used to go ballistic when she would bring home name-brand "Science Diet" food for the dogs' meals, while he was given "Plain Wrap" brand beer. It literally just said "BEER" in generic block letters on the side of the can. My dad hated that stuff. He called it donkey piss. That always made me laugh as a kid. Nonetheless, there was no debate as to the lineup of our household. There was a distinct hierarchy as far as my mother was concerned, and it went as follows: Her husband, Toby, Annabelle, Starbelle, Cooper, and then me. Some would argue that I ranked just between my father and Toby, and to be fair, I am sure that is true. But from my perspective as a youngster, this is the order that I felt was legitimate at the time.

You might wonder why Toby was at the top of the canine ranking list. I often did. I mean, Annabelle and her offspring were heir to greatness after all. Now, I always figured Cooper was last in line (behind his mother and sister) due to the fact that he was *special*. That's how my mother always referred to Cooper after he would shit, one more time, on the living room carpet.

"He's *special,* Annabelle," she would exclaim while she was, yet again, on her hands and knees, scrubbing the floor with a wooden brush and disinfectant solution.

I later came to find out that Cooper was actually born dead on our kitchen linoleum. It wasn't until I was much older that I learned that my mother, in a true angelic gesture, revived Cooper from certain peril. My mother begged my father to breed Annabelle one time in order to extend the presidential bloodline. Begrudgingly, my father acquiesced. Apparently, in her preparations to become the canine midwife to presidential royalty, she read in a book somewhere that sometimes dogs will, like humans, deliver a stillborn offspring. However, in some rare cases, stillborn puppies can be revived by rubbing them vigorously between your palms as if rubbing your hands together for warmth. As family legend has it, Cooper was born dead, Mom rubbed him vigorously between her hands, and life was restored. A *miracle* puppy he would be called. Unfortunately, this miracle dog never learned to lift his leg to pee, nor did he even learn to go outside to relieve himself. He also had chronically bad breath, fetid ears, severe allergies which required daily medication, and a wickedly pronounced underbite. Ah yes, he was *special* indeed.

But still... why did Toby, a mutt no less, rank above Liberty Lady's Annabelle and her spawn? I later came to realize it was not because of his ancestry. Rather, it was because of his gender. He was male. Growing up in the 1970 and 80s taught me several "truths" about life, and one of the most prominent and profound was that men were more important than women. Period. Consequently, this belief propelled what became my decades-long search for "Mr. Right." If there was one thing my mother instilled in me from the time I was a very young girl, it was that a woman is only as important, powerful, or significant as her husband. She often told me, "Annabelle, remember this: your husband will make the living, but you, his wife, will make his life *worth* living." I sort of found that funny as I glanced over to my dad angrily choking down his "BEER." But she wasn't the only person to remind me that men were something to be sought after, cherished, honored, and revered. This idea was echoed repeatedly throughout society; I was reminded of this "truth" in Sunday school, in regular school, on TV shows, in movies, in magazines, in the homes of my friends and family, and so on. It was in the air we breathed and in the food we ate. It was all around us and within us, and I, like many of my brethren, became consumed by it.

I remember this message with the clarity of a recovered alcoholic. Now, think about this: If that were the case for me in the 1970s and 80s, I have to imagine that what my mother experienced in the 1950s and 60s was even more extreme. Though she occasionally made fleeting comments about dreams she had as a young girl to become a famous singer, I can only imagine those dreams seemed unrealistic and futile. How could she become a renowned singer and entertainer if she was far too busy finding and then tending to a man?

It is a pity, though. She truly had a magnificent voice. She had one of those voices that just soothed your soul. She was also incredibly beautiful. Her nickname in high school was Helen. You know, like Helen of Troy... whose face launched a thousand ships. When I was a child, she regularly sang me lullabies as I drifted off to sleep in my Wonder Woman jammies under my Care Bears comforter. If I suffered a booboo or a heartbreak, she could miraculously take away any pain I was experiencing by softly singing Christine McVie's "Songbird" from Fleetwood Mac's *Rumors* album. This song soothed my tears away and made me feel like the most loved person in the world.

Car rides were particularly magical for me as a kid. We would sing our favorite songs at the top of our lungs, windows down, wind racing through our hair. Mom would teach me when to take breaths, how to harmonize, and why to use just the right amount of vibrato. She also introduced me to some of the greatest music, made by some of the most influential female artists, the world has ever known. I often found it interesting that she seemed to worship these singers. I often wondered, *how did they make it work, Mom, and why couldn't you?* Among our favorite songs were "It's Too Late" and "So Far Away" from Carole

King's *Tapestry* album and Joni Mitchell's *Blue* album. We particularly loved "Carey" and "River." Singing with my mom was possibly the only time I felt like I *really* knew her. Or, like I knew the *real* her. Despite our occasional disputes and our regular disagreements, I idolized my mother.

I loved to visualize my mom as a carefree young woman, enrapturing crowds with her mesmerizing voice and captivating, good looks. I wondered if she had these fantasies too. Were those dreams thwarted by the expectations of *her* society? Or by the expectations of *her* mother? When I would ask her why she didn't pursue a life of music, she would fall silent for a moment and then, as if she were working up the courage to confront that memory, she would reply, "Oh, Annabelle. What kind of wife and mother would I be if I had a life like that?"

Though, I would often catch her singing deeply moving ballads while simultaneously looking off into the distance with a sense of something sad or lost. One of her favorite songs to sing was "Killing Me Softly" by the incomparable Roberta Flack. Many view this beautiful song as a lament for a failed or unrequited love relationship between a man and a woman. For Mom, it felt like it was a love letter to her unmanifested musical career. To this day, I still tear up and feel a lump growing in my throat when I hear that song. Was it longing I heard reverberating in my mother's beautiful voice as she belted out those soulful lyrics? Was it regret?

Despite any personal ambitions my mother may have given up in her own life, she wasn't about to let me live mine in any way that would compromise my commitment to satisfying social norms. She was determined to help me fetch myself a man. Truly, I needed to keep my eyes set squarely on the prize. I had *one* job as a budding young woman: find my "Prince Charming." I bought into this notion, and I made it my life's mission to succeed. Regardless of any teenaged angst I may have displayed, the last thing I wanted to do was disappoint my mother or fail in my prime objective. I had always heard that if you kiss enough toads, you will eventually find your prince. For better or for worse, what follows in this manuscript details that very quest.

Chapter 1: Oz

I grew up in Southern California in a small, quiet suburb. I spent my childhood participating in "normal," gender-appropriate activities. I had several girlfriends who lived on my block, and we spent most of our free time together. Sure, there were boys on my street as well. But honestly, why would we ever play with them? On warm days, we played outside in our yards and in the cul-de-sac until the streetlights came on. One of our favorite activities was putting on mock wedding ceremonies in our driveways. We used lace doilies from the kitchen as veils, and we picked the neighbor's roses for our bouquets. We practiced walking down the aisle… you know, that weird processional gait where you step with the left foot, then bring the right foot to it…. Then step with the right foot, and then bring the left foot to it. We would talk for hours about what colors our bridesmaids would be wearing (my go-to was always dusty rose and vanilla), and what song we would play for our first dance (I had my little-kid heart set on "How Deep Is Your Love" by the Bee Gees). During the evenings, or on those rare occasions when it was too cold or rainy to go outside, we would play in one of our homes. We played with our Easy Bake Ovens, our Fashion Plates, and our Barbie dolls. We practiced cooking and looking fabulous; our training for wife-life and motherhood started early. It picked up steam, naturally, in high school.

I wouldn't say those four years of high school were the "best years of my life," but they weren't the worst either. Mostly, I kept myself busy with dance team, drama class, and maintaining social capital. School work came easily to me, and I had plenty of friends. I wouldn't say that I was the *most* popular girl in school, but I definitely felt like I was part of the "in crowd." I also took my husband hunt with more skepticism than my mom would have liked. Mother regularly reminded me that she met *her* Prince Charming (also known to me as "Dad") in high school. There was no reason, she would argue, that I would need to do anything differently. Although that I believed my parents had as idyllic a relationship as was likely possible, I still remained a little skeptical that high school was the best pool from which to select a life partner.

Nonetheless, despite my own personal apprehension about committing to a boy who could potentially become my husband while still so young, I did have one boyfriend throughout the entirety of high school. To be specific, I guess you could call him "on again, off again," but he was mostly "on." We met just as our freshman year was starting, and we dated until we graduated four years later. Sure, we would have the occasional blowout dispute that would inevitably end in one of us declaring "That's it! We are through!" But, within a week or two, we found our way back to one another to give it another go.

I am not exactly sure what kept us coming back together all those years. At the time, I naively suspected it could be fate. I had the romantic notion that we might have been *destined* to be together.... Soulmates whose hearts were entwined, inexplicably, endlessly. For him, I assume he just liked having a girl who was always there for him. I provided many conveniences and perks: For one, I was a girl with whom he could consistently have sex (well, as consistently as was possible for two kids who lived in their parents' homes). We basically fornicated, every once in a while, in the backseat of his Oldsmobile. This would probably be reason number one for any teenaged boy to stay in a relationship. In addition to virtually unlimited access to sex, I also let him copy off my homework and tests in class. This was particularly convenient, as I was a straight-A student, and he was... well... let's just say, he struggled. If these advantages weren't enough, when we turned 16 years old, I was the designated driver who safely ushered him to and fro while he and his buddies got shit-faced at whatever house party we attended. So, yeah. I suppose I was quite handy indeed.

His name was Jeremy, but people called him Oz because he was a self-proclaimed devotee of the hardcore rocker Ozzy Osbourne. He was the classic 80s heavy metal guy who donned black eyeliner, black nail polish, and studded belts and bracelets. He wore his hair long and unkempt, and he uttered phrases like: "I wanna rock!" at random and inappropriate times. Though, despite our differences (he the diehard metal head; me the strait-laced cheerleader), I simply thought he was *super cool*. I also thought I would be the one to change him, to *tame the wild stallion* as it were. I think I watched one too many John Hughes films.

So, yes, high school is really where this quest to find my Prince Charming sincerely began. It's such an unrealistic pursuit if you think about it. What are the chances that I could find my valiant prince among the tendrils of the acne-ridden, hormone-raging halls of a California high school? Even though it was a private, parochial school, I think I'd be lucky to find a half-baked *squire* if we're being honest. But, hey, I found Oz.

If my mother's consistent encouragement wasn't enough, my high school itself also reinforced this notion that we should be in hot pursuit of a life partner. We had a school-wide activity where the seniors each had to find a partner of the opposite sex to marry. The teachers held a pseudo wedding ceremony in the gymnasium, and the principal pronounced us "high school husband and wife." Looking back, I am sure it was quite a nauseating spectacle. All the girls dressed up in their finest white dresses, and the boys wore their best shirts and slacks. Gossip spread hither and tither about who was "marrying" whom, and relationships were strained and tested. Naturally, Oz and I paired up for this activity. Thinking back on it now, I wonder what they did if there was an odd number of kids in the class? Would the leftover person need to "marry" a teacher? *Woof. Nauseating.* I can't imagine they would sanction a polygamist arrangement. And what if the genders were not equally split? There was no way the Christian high school principal would permit a homosexual marital arrangement. Auspiciously, I was immune to these details at that time. As a typically self-absorbed teenaged girl, I had my "husband" in hand, so I was personally set. There was no need to concern myself with the others. Nonetheless, I am sure it was less than ideal for several poor students who didn't have a partner on lockdown.

In any event, a few weeks after the wedding, each couple was granted a "miracle." This miracle was anywhere from one to three raw eggs. These eggs simulated babies. It was our job to name, gender, and decorate these children. Then, we had to care for them over the next couple of months. The principal marked each egg with a special stamp so that he would know if we broke it and tried to substitute it with a replacement egg. Yes, he had his bases covered. Furthermore, we had to take our "kids" with us everywhere... to class, to practice, to various school outings, and home for the night. We were even supposed to take the eggs to our various weekend activities. However, if my classmates were like me, those eggs definitely stayed in our bedrooms. Why risk breaking your egg at the mall on Saturday afternoon if the principal's prying eyes were not there? If your egg broke, you failed the assignment. *What kind of parents will you be one day if you can't even keep an egg in one piece*? the teachers would chide. Besides, can you imagine how embarrassing that would be to drop a raw egg that hadn't been refrigerated for weeks? Dreadful.

As luck would have it, Oz and I were blessed with just *one* miracle. I honestly felt sorry for the "parents" of triplets. That was three times the work and three times the likelihood of disaster. Oz and I decided our "baby" was a girl, and we named her Cory, short for Corinthians. We hoped we may get extra credit for naming the baby after a book of the Bible. Spoiler alert: we didn't. Nonetheless, we completed the assignment in earnest. We decorated her with spurts of blonde hair, simulated by gluing on pieces of shorn yellow yarn. We painted on big blue eyes, and we carried her around on a little blanket in an Easter basket that simulated a makeshift baby carriage.

Unsurprisingly, I did the lion's share of the work on this project. I never even let Oz take Cory home with him at night. I was not about to jeopardize my perfect academic record by putting him in charge of that egg. He certainly didn't protest either. Ironically, neither one of us thought twice about the injustice of the situation. Frankly, it seemed perfectly natural. Moms are supposed to be in charge of babies, right? I am sure most of my classmates had similar arrangements. Yes, thanks to me, the egg survived its two-month childhood, and we earned an A on the project. Mom was proud. I could see a glimmer of hope in her eyes that this assignment really touched my soul and made me realize how important and exciting it would be to become a mother. Another spoiler alert: it didn't.

***

Looking back, Even though I was undoubtedly enamored, Oz really was a bit of a dud. It's not just because he didn't pull his weight with the egg project. Sure, he was good looking, popular, and played in a rock band (the high school trifecta). Unfortunately, he was also a budding alcoholic who had no observable life goals other than maintaining his hard rock lifestyle and sleeping with anything with a pulse. Quite honestly, people always asked me why I stayed with him.

"He's a louse, Annabelle! What do you see in him?" my parents would demand.

What did I see in him? I saw what most other teenaged girls saw: a bad boy with a guitar slung over his shoulder and piercing blue eyes. Was this a trick question?

Despite his dubious nature, my parents still allowed me to date him. Sure, they would have preferred that I selected a boy with more "potential" as they saw it, but given the choice of either dating Oz or remaining single, they certainly preferred Oz.

We had some family friends who had a daughter my age named Danielle. Danielle dated a boy named Charles who wore slacks and button-up shirts to school. He played the French horn, dutifully executed his paper route each weekend, and built model airplanes in his parents' garage.

"Why can't *you* find a nice boy like Charles?" my mother would demand.

"A guy like Charles?" I would feign vomiting, "Oh my God, Mom. No way! Gross. Gag me with a spoon! Nerd-alert!" In 1980s teenage vernacular, that was a "hard no."

The thought of dating someone like Charles was as repugnant to my 17-year-old sensibilities as it would have been to date a bridge troll.

The joke might have been on me, however. Turns out, Charles became the CEO of a fortune-500 company, and Danielle is currently sitting pretty in her 5,000 square foot home in Malibu. Nonetheless, I wouldn't have dated Charles back then if my life literally depended on it.

"It's important for a young woman to have a male companion, Annabelle. You need to start learning what it is like to be in a relationship," my mother would advise.

Despite the fact that they were less than approving of my choice in Oz, I can remember my parents going out of their way to make sure that he felt welcome and comfortable in our home. My mother would virtually roll out the red carpet every time he was over.

"May I get you something cold to drink, Oz?" She would fuss and fawn over him to make sure he had the best slice of meatloaf on the table and that his glass of seltzer never ran dry.

As soon as he left, I would marvel at her droning on and on about how he is a sincere disappointment and that I could do so much better.

"Well, you could have fooled me, Mom. You hung on every word that he said, and you treated him like a king!"

"Well, Annabelle, he is your suitor, after all. I may not consider him to be the *best* suitor you could possibly find, but he is certainly better than *nothing*!" She would throw her hands in the air and storm off as if she were frustrated by everything.

So, there it was. Whether or not she intended to, Mom trained me to believe that being with a substandard male partner was better than going it alone. Forget the fact that he continually disrespected me. Never mind that he had zero life ambition. He had a penis, for God's sake.

I remember one particularly nasty fight that Oz and I endured. Oz had, once again, cheated on me with another girl at school. I heard they were spotted making out on the football field, behind the snack shack. I was devastated, and I felt as though my heart might never recover. Yes, my 17-year-old life had hit rock bottom, it seemed. I was moping around the house for days, and my mom was starting to worry because I wasn't snapping out of it. This was one benefit of having an overbearing, stay-at-home mother: she was always keenly aware of what I was going through, and she never let me suffer alone. To cheer me up, one Saturday afternoon, she decided to take me shopping at the mall. We hit our favorite stores: Contempo Casuals, Judy's, and Miller's Outpost. Mom loved to buy me clothes and was quick to tell me how beautiful I looked in every outfit.

"Oh, Annabelle!" she would gasp, "You look absolutely stunning. You should definitely get that white mini skirt! Oz will have no choice but to take you back when he sees you wearing it!"

Although I should have been extremely insulted that my mother would want me to wear a skimpy outfit just so that I could be "taken back" by this boy she had many times admitted was substandard, I didn't seem to notice that it was in any way problematic. Instead, I was flattered, and she gave me hope that we would indeed reunite. Besides, I sincerely appreciated my mother's validation and her attempts to bolster my self-confidence. Honestly, our relationship was complicated, though I suspect it was very much par for the course. Sure, we fought in the way that many mothers quarrel with their teenaged daughters, but, despite it all, I sincerely loved my mother, and I desperately needed her support and her love. I particularly craved her approval. She was always there for me when I was in a pickle. Always. Whether she would sing me a sweet lullaby when I was feeling down or take me to the mall to shop 'til we dropped, Mom consistently showed up for me. And this time, once again, our little retail therapy session worked to improve my morose mood.

On the way out of the mall, upbeat and hopeful that my relationship with Oz would be back on track in no time, I begged my mom to stop in for a moment at a little store called Spencer's Gifts. This was a quirky little shop that sold off-beat gag gifts, pop culture products, and irreverent trinkets. Quick to keep my spirits up, Mom agreed. She didn't necessarily know what she was getting into when we entered the establishment, but she quickly realized it was quite inappropriate.

Holding up a festive red and blue box that held a little plastic turd in it, Mother cried, "Why on earth would someone buy this?"

"I don't know," I replied, absently, "maybe to give it to someone you don't like?"

"Well, that is just ridiculous, Annabelle. Why would someone spend their hard-earned dollars to purchase poop in a box for someone they don't like?" She seemed flabbergasted by the mere notion.

"Mom, who knows!? But anyway, who cares. I just want to buy some new stickers for my notebook."

"Ugh, fine, Annabelle. But please hurry. I don't want to be caught dead in here. Imagine if one of my church friends stopped in. I would be humiliated!"

"Mom, if one of your church friends stopped in, then that means they too shop here. So, no need to be embarrassed!"

To this airtight rationale, Mother just rolled her eyes and said, "Please, Annabelle. Just select your stickers quickly."

I launched my sticker hunt in earnest. Back then, it was popular to cover your Trapper Keeper with trendy stickers. I couldn't use the same ones my peers had, however. I needed to be unique. I found many contenders, but Mom said I had to narrow it down to three. After abundant and thoughtful consideration, I decided to purchase the following: a "Save Ferris" sticker memorializing the hit film *Ferris Bueller's Day Off,* a sticker of a little alien that said "ET Phone Home" commemorating the Spielberg classic *ET,* and a sticker that read "No Fat Chicks" with a picture of a rooster holding a sign that displayed a heavy-set chicken with a red circle and line through it.

Mom thought these selections were sensible, and we stepped up to the cash register to buy the treasures.

"Cool stickers," the teenaged, male cashier mentioned. "I love the 'No Fat Chicks' one. It makes you think it's all about not wanting to have fat chickens, but it's really about not wanting to have fat girls."

"Yeah," I replied, sluggishly. "Totally."

I remember feeling a little bit sick as he bagged the stickers and handed me the merchandise. As Mother and I got into the car to head back home, I asked her if the chicken sticker was mean.

"Mean?" she repeated. "What do you mean by mean?" She seemed genuinely stumped.

"I just mean, is it mean...? You know, is it rude.... to have a sticker that is basically saying that fat girls are bad?" I had a hard time putting this simple yet profound thought into words.

"No, Annabelle. It is not mean." She reasoned. "Look, it's just the reality of life that men prefer slender women."

This rationale appeared to be perfectly logical to her.

"I know, Mom, but it kinda makes me feel bad. Maybe I shouldn't put it on my notebook after all." I suddenly felt a heavy weight in my chest.

"Oh, for heaven's sake, Annabelle," my mother replied, "Why would you feel bad? You are slender, dear. You have nothing to worry about. And as for the fact that men prefer lean women, that's just the way it is. It's a simple fact. There's nothing for you to feel bad about. You didn't make that rule. It's just life."

Despite my mother's reasoning, I couldn't bring myself to affix the chicken sticker on my folder. Back then, I didn't have the vocabulary to explain why this kind of messaging was problematic. I couldn't explain how these images were degrading to all women, regardless of their body shape, and that to reduce a woman's value down to her physical figure is demoralizing and misogynistic. All I could say was it made me feel icky. I ended up shoving the sticker under my bed among other random and forgettable items. Oddly, I couldn't bring myself to throw it away (perhaps because I was taught by my thrifty parents to never dispose of items that are still usable), but I also couldn't display it on my folder. Thus, it found its way into the abyss beneath my bed.

Interestingly, as a side note, I found this sticker a couple of years ago. It had apparently been shoved at some point between the pages of my freshman high school yearbook. I was cleaning out the garage one day, and I came across my old annuals. I opened this one, and out popped that sticker.

My face immediately grew red with both embarrassment and anger. I was proud that my 17-year-old self didn't ultimately display that image, but my 45-year-old self was furious that it even existed… and that I purchased it… and that I never destroyed it.

On Monday morning, I went back to school, Trapper Keeper in hand (donning only the ET and Ferris Bueller stickers), wearing my brand new white mini skirt and a multi-colored MTV t-shirt. Predictably, Oz came running back to me, promising that he had made his final mistake. *Mom was right,* I thought to myself. *The white mini skirt worked.*

This cycle of date for a few months, break up for a few days, date for a few months played on repeat until we graduated. Despite our proclamations of staying "together forever," we broke up for good after I went away to college. Sure, we said we'd remain a couple and endure the semi-long distance, but within weeks of my departure, he was on to new, local girls, and, frankly, I was preoccupied with the new stable of "college men." So, in the end, the split was amicable.

Looking back, if you were to ask me if I regret the time I spent with Oz, I would answer with a resounding "Hell no!" For all the heartache and drama he may have caused through our tumultuous four-year relationship, he gave me the best part of high school as well: he gave me Sophie.

Chapter 2: Sophie

Sophie lived next door to Oz, and the two had known each other since birth. Their parents had been best friends back in college, so Sophie was more like a sister to Oz than a neighbor or even a family friend. Their families vacationed together and spent holidays together. Many people actually believed they were related. Although never romantically involved (each would separately tell me that the thought of hooking up with one another was a repulsive notion, akin to sleeping with your sibling), Oz and Sophie were very, very close.

One time I asked Sophie why she never considered dating Oz. She looked at me, bewildered, as though she were about to vomit.

"Um, I don't know, Annie," she replied sarcastically. "Why don't you want to date your brother?"

"Easy, I don't have any brothers, Sophie," I replied with smug satisfaction.

"Well, imagine dating your own father, and then double the amount of disgust because, unlike your father, you have actually seen your brother eat his own scabs as a child."

Ok, she won that argument.

When I started dating Oz, Sophie and I became fast friends. I was with her nearly every day of high school, whether or not Oz was there with us as well. Although 5 months my junior, I looked up to Sophie as if she were an esteemed elder. She was really everything I was not; she was assertive, self-confident, and bold. While I think some people would have considered me to be those things too, that really wasn't the truth. Those who knew me very well (like Sophie), knew that I was, at heart, a very co-dependent person. I drew my sense of self-worth from making other people feel happy and satisfied. This can prove to be a dangerous cocktail for a young woman coming of age in the 1970s and 80s. Fortunately, because of Sophie (or "Soph" as I call her), I was eventually able to find my own voice and my own value.

Another difference between Soph and me was our family structure. Sophie was the oldest of five siblings: two younger sisters and two younger brothers. They are of Italian descent, and their loud, boisterous nature was overshadowed only by their deep love for one another. Her parents were also fairly wealthy (at least by middle-class, suburban standards) and socially connected in our city. As owners of the most popular Italian restaurant in town, everyone knew them. Sophie's parents were essentially local royalty. She also had a handful of aunts, uncles, and cousins who lived nearby and would spend plenty of time at her house. Weekends and holidays at Sophie's were always amazing spectacles to behold. There was constantly so much going on: people rushing in and out, parties taking place, hands flying as they spoke a mile a minute, and new pieces of family drama beginning and ending. On the other hand, my house was the complete opposite. Although it was a loving and peaceful home, I was an only child of two introverted parents who happened to be only-children themselves. In this way, my house could be aptly summed up by an average teenager in one word: boring.

As a typical eldest sibling, Sophie had a lot of experience with babysitting and taking care of the house. Her parents worked at their restaurant most evenings and on weekends, so Sophie was left in charge at home. This responsibility gave Sophie a level of confidence that I would take many years to develop. She was equally comfortable with changing diapers as she was with calling a plumber to come and fix the sink that was leaking. Her skillset never ceased to amaze me. She could seamlessly juggle putting her baby sisters down for a nap while simultaneously studying for her chemistry test. I could barely manage to get myself dressed for school in the morning, so I was truly in awe of Sophie's maturity and ability to simply get shit done.

Mother loved that I spent a lot of time at Sophie's house. She seemed optimistic that Sophie's domestic abilities would somehow rub off on me. She would regularly tease me for not being as capable or resourceful as Sophie.

"Oh, Annabelle. That Sophie is simply amazing. What a wonderful wife and mother she will become! She was born to raise children, that one. You can just tell. And, my word! Does she sure know her way around a kitchen. You would be wise to follow her example, darling," she would nudge.

Although I couldn't disagree with my mother's assessment of Sophie's capabilities, I always found it a little insulting and frankly absurd that she would compare us in this way. How was I supposed to practice these domestic skills in a home with no other children and a mother who micromanaged every piece of the household operation? Nonetheless, I would never argue with her because that deep admiration of Sophie meant that Mother would never prevent me from spending time at her house. Mom got to imagine me in the greatest domestic training forum on the face of the planet, and I got to hang out with my best friend. *It's a win-win,* I figured.

Despite our minor differences, Soph and I were completely inseparable throughout high school. She was my best friend, my confidant, and my support system. Whom did I call when I caught Oz cheating on me, *again,* with another girl at school? I called Soph. Whom did I consult when I needed to select a new outfit to wear to school that would simultaneously intimidate said other girl and also make Oz sorry he screwed things up me with yet again and leave him with no other possible alternative than to beg for me back into his suddenly worthless and empty existence? I consulted Soph. At times, she was my biggest ally and Oz' worst nightmare. She would warn Oz that he had better shape up and treat me right or she would tell his parents about the bag of marijuana she knew he had hidden inside the hollowed-out Bible he kept on the top shelf of his closet. Since they had grown up together so closely, she knew exactly how to hit Oz where it hurt. Despite the occasional Oz drama, Sophie and I really had the time of our lives in high school.

Weekends with Sophie were always exciting. I used to spend the night at Sophie's house almost every Friday or Saturday night. Mother was thrilled for me to be there, in the classroom of Sophie's home. It was Home-Ec 101. I am surprised Mother never asked me to take notes. In addition to the fact that I was witness to considerable domestic training, Sophie and I would also entertain ourselves in cheeky and irreverent ways. I am a little embarrassed to admit that one of our favorite activities was telling her little brothers ghost stories, and then laughing wildly as they ran into their bedrooms to hide under their beds. We would stand just outside of their bedroom moaning and scratching on the door as they shrieked in terror. On the lighter side, we would often ask her little sisters to take action photos of us with the Polaroid camera as we would leap errantly from the family room couch and attempt to strike a crazy pose, mid-air. They usually only caught a foot, or maybe half a leg, or even a blurry midsection, but we loved to try over and over until we ran out of film.

In addition to these random activities, we also spent considerable time tending to the house and children. To be fair, the only cooking I ever learned to do was at Sophie's house. She taught me how to boil pasta, toast garlic bread in the oven, and even make homemade tomato sauce from scratch. We would usually cook using leftover ingredients from the restaurant, and then we would feed the kids and ourselves our creations. After cleaning up the dinner dishes, we would help her sisters and brothers take baths and brush their teeth, and then we would tuck them into their beds. Her sisters shared a room with two twin beds in it. Their beds were suspended in white metal frames with decorative headboards that donned metallic pink and red roses. The walls were painted Pepto-Bismol pink, and the room was essentially decorated to look like a magical land. There were posters of butterflies and fairies on their walls, more stuffed animals than you could count, and colorful unicorn comforters on their beds. Her brothers shared a room with brown, wooden bunk beds. Their room was decorated in a sports motif. The wallpaper had different types of sporting equipment—basketballs, footballs, soccer balls, tennis rackets, baseballs, and hockey sticks—and there was a tabletop lamp with a baseball bat for the base and a baseball glove turned upside down as the lampshade. If you weren't careful, you were likely to step on a matchbox car or an action figure that had been haphazardly strewn across the floor.

Fortunately, Sophie had her own room. She had a trundle bed, so I was able to sleep there when I stayed over. Her bedroom was decorated as a typical high school girl would decorate it in the 1980s. She had a rainbow throw rug atop her brown, shag carpeted floor. Her little bedside table held a small, framed, needlepoint picture that boasted a big yellow smiley face that read "Have a Nice Day." She made that in summer camp when she was younger, and she considered it to be a fine work of art. She also had a phone in her room with her own, private phone number that was separate from her parents' line. I was green with envy. Her walls donned dozens of unframed posters and photographs. She had an *Outsiders* poster on one wall, surrounded by a bunch of our Polaroid photos held up by thumb tacks. She had a couple of different Wham! posters on another wall, and a *Purple Rain* poster on the third wall. The main attraction, however, were the rows and rows of cassette tapes stacked up along the fourth wall. She had all the best cassettes in her collection: Culture Club, Billy Idol, Prince, Thompson Twins, New Order, Michael Jackson, Madonna, Duran Duran, Depeche Mode, Whitesnake, The Bangles, The Cure, and Foreigner (to name a few). We would spend hours listening to those cassettes, singing along at the top of our lungs, trying to memorize the lyrics. We would study the printed lyrics that lined the inner walls of the cassette cases, working hard to commit every word to memory like it was our full-time job.

Once tucked into their beds, Sophie would read her sisters a story while I would read a story to her brothers. While her sisters usually demanded a classic fairytale or a Disney Princess book, her brothers preferred adventure stories about dinosaurs or pirates. Once the littles were down for the count, we would stay up late, eat ice cream, listen to music, crank call random people from school, or watch an R-rated movie. This time of autonomy was ecstasy for me. At my house, I couldn't sneeze without my mother hearing it and rushing in to make sure I wasn't coming down with something. At Sophie's house, we were free to do as we pleased. It's true that tending to her siblings was indeed a bit of a chore and an obligation. Making dinners, helping with bedtime routines, and tending to the house was a heavy responsibility; however, the freedom to do as we pleased once the children went to bed was simply exhilarating and definitely worth any hassle the rest of it had produced. Her parents would come home very, very late, well after the little ones had gone to bed. As soon as we heard the garage door opening, Sophie and I would stop whatever we were doing, race into her bedroom, and bury ourselves under the covers, pretending we were already asleep. Her parents would dutifully peek into each of the bedrooms to check on their children and whisper goodnight. I loved when they would peer into Sophie's room. They would bring in the most delicious smells from the restaurant. To this day, when I get a whiff of garlic and oregano, my mind immediately takes me back to Sophie's childhood home.

Some of Soph and my other favorite pastimes, when not tending to her young siblings and singing along to her cassette tapes, included typical high school activities such as thumbing through our high school yearbooks, identifying the cutest boys we would love to go out with and the boys we would only date on a dare; prancing around shamelessly, in our bikinis, taking turns striking alluring poses and snapping photos of ourselves with her Polaroid camera; playing the latest Madonna album at full blast in her bedroom and dancing around seductively, trying to master the "come hither" look; or caking on every manner of cosmetics onto our fresh and wrinkle-free faces and teasing our hair with a rat tail comb and some Aqua Net to make us look like the latest cover of *Cosmo* magazine.

Sophie and I complemented each other perfectly. I was a blonde; she was a brunette. I had blue eyes; she had brown. I liked to wear pastel colors; she preferred jewel tones. I liked to talk about people I didn't care for behind their backs and snipe them with passive-aggressive quips; she liked to cuss people out directly to their face. We truly went together like cream and coffee.

Sophie had a few boyfriends throughout high school, but none of them ever really stuck. She would often complain that she couldn't keep a guy if her life depended on it. She maintained her self-confidence, however, and merely chalked it up to the fickle nature of high school boys. She consistently kept her head up and remained convinced that her dating odds would improve in college. While I would agree that teenagers can, for the most part, be considered capricious, I would also argue that Sophie scared the shit out of these boys. She was a headstrong young woman who knew what she wanted, and she never held back her opinions; that's intimidating for any young soul. Those poor high school boys didn't stand a chance.

Although Sophie and I fancied ourselves the slightly younger versions of Laverne and Shirley, our high school classmates started calling us Kelly and Lisa. I was Kelly, and Sophie was Lisa. They were basically terms of endearment (I think). The name Kelly referred to Kelly Bundy from a brand-new, popular television sitcom called *Married with Children.* Kelly Bundy was played by the witty and talented Christina Applegate. Kelly (like me) wore her bleached-blonde hair teased and tousled, with enormous bangs that reached out to the sky. At the time, I was sincerely flattered to be compared to Kelly Bundy, as I found this character to be extremely attractive and savagely witty. Looking back, however, I am not so convinced it was a compliment. It would be inaccurate to say that Kelly was the brightest crayon in the box or that she exuded modesty. On the contrary, we could safely assert that she was mentally and sexually unencumbered and leave it at that.

Sophie, on the other hand, was compared to Lisa, the homemade, would-be sex robot (played by the alluring Kelly LeBrock) in the 1985 comedy/sci-fi hit film, *Weird Science*. Like Lisa, Sophie had long brown hair and sultry bedroom eyes; more importantly, she carried herself in the same confident way that Lisa did. She didn't take shit from anyone, and she regularly put idiot teenaged boys in their place. All things considered, I would say that being compared to Lisa was much more flattering than being compared to Kelly. But, at the time, we both relished our monikers.

Looking back, though our hair and eye color differed, and we approached life with slightly different perspectives, we certainly also had quite a lot in common. When I reflect on it now, I realize that even our favorite activities back then (namely, prancing and primping) ultimately involved trying, desperately, to reel in that ultimate *whale* of a prize. Prince Charming, it turns out, was our Moby Dick.

Unsurprisingly, when it came time to finish up our high school careers and begin to consider our college options, we decided upon two, non-negotiable conditions: we would only go to college if we could 1) go to the same school and 2) live together. After four years of near inseparability, daily college life without each other in it seemed bleak and unrealistic. Although Sophie's parents would surely miss her support at home, they fortunately endorsed our plans to go away to college. My parents, too, supported our intentions. Who else would they want their daughter to be aligned with in college other than the perfect wife and mother in-the-making? Further, we both made good grades in high school, so we could basically name our university. And, as history reveals, that's what we did. We applied together, were accepted together, and left high school together… knowing that the next four-years in college would be spent in the ultimate pursuit of our lives, college men.

Chapter 3: Dormies

Despite my occasional lack of focus and my less-than-optimal study habits, I always seemed to make good grades, and I actually enjoyed learning. I did quite well in high school, and, as a result, I made it into to a top university. Gratefully, I had Soph by my side. As college students, finally away from home, we were anxious to have the time of our lives. We went away to school not only to learn about our respective academic fields, but to grow into the bona fide adults we always longed to be. We were eager to meet new people and expand our social horizons.

Like most freshman starting college for the first time, Sophie and I lived in a dorm. While some of our high school peers were able to swing an off-campus apartment right out of the gate, Sophie and I lacked both the funds as well as the parental support to accomplish such a feat. So, we settled for an on-campus dorm. There were five on-campus dormitories at our university, and each of them were named after famous California cities or natural landmarks. We had Catalina, San Francisco, Joshua Tree, Yosemite, and Big Sur. We were placed into Big Sur, which was the largest and most expensive of the bunch. It's not that our parents wanted to pay the extra fee for this particular building, but it just so happened that it was the only dorm where you could guarantee that you would be placed with someone you knew and requested. As rooming with Sophie was a non-negotiable condition, our parents acquiesced and coughed up the extra couple hundred bucks a year to make it happen. However, paying the even *steeper* price for an off-campus apartment was out of the question. So, we happily settled for Big Sur, or "BS" as the inhabitants lovingly referred to it. We called our fellow dorm-dwellers "dormies," and we definitely made the most of our time there.

While BS did guarantee that Sophie and I were able to share a room, we also had two randomly placed "suitemates" right next door. Our two rooms were separated by a tiny bathroom that the four of us shared. While suddenly going from an only child who had the luxury of having an en suite bathroom exclusively to herself to sharing a miniscule restroom with three other women was a shock, I relished every minute of it. It felt like we were living in a two-bedroom, one-bathroom apartment, though this "apartment" was exceptionally small. The bedroom consisted of two twin beds, two small desks with tiny bookshelves attached to the back of them, and one small closet that held maybe 30 articles of clothing, and four small drawers. That was it. There was obviously no living room or kitchen. Honestly, this entire dorm room was smaller than either one of our bedrooms back home, and we had to share it. Nonetheless, this was the closest thing to real adulting we had ever done, and we couldn't have been happier to be there. Plus, unlike the other four dorms on campus, we were lucky enough to be placed into the one that had semi-private bathrooms like this. All of the other dormitories had one massive restroom per floor that had to be shared by dozens of women. I was grateful for this 4:1 ratio.

Unlike Sophie and me, our next-door neighbor suitemates did not know each other before they were paired up as roommates. Although most rooms were occupied by friends who applied to room together, this was not exclusively the case. Both of our suitemates requested Big Sur because they had extra money to spend, and they wanted to lock in the semi-private bathroom situation. One of the roommates was named Genevieve. Gen hailed from an upper-class suburb of Atlanta, Georgia. The daughter of a politician father and a socialite mother, Gen had a thick, Southern drawl, and a taste for the finer things in life. She grew up in a huge plantation home that boasted dozens of rooms and a vast, rolling yard made up of several acres. When she first arrived at Big Sur, she was pleased to find out that she was placed on the top (fifth) floor. "Oh, thank goodness, Daddy," I heard her tell her father in sincere relief, "the penthouse suite!" Little did she know that living on the top floor only meant a longer commute to and from the exit of the building via the ancient elevator that was always packed or sometimes out of order, or the stairwell that was creepy and smelled like a mixture of cigarette smoke and mildew.

Despite the fact that she was crammed into her dorm room just like the rest of us, she always seemed to resemble someone who just stepped out of a *Southern Living* magazine. Gen was tall and slender, and she wore her light brown hair in long waves past her shoulders. Her attire was always impeccable. Her clothing was stylish and chic, and she took great pride in the fact that she knew the difference between haute couture and luxury fashion. She wouldn't dream of wearing anything off a sale rack, and she certainly didn't own any sneakers. She was also as oddly prim and proper as any 18-year-old young woman could possibly be. Consequently, she found dorm life to be quite daunting, indeed. She was constantly droning on and on about etiquette, manners, and proper social protocol.

"Would you mind not throwing your towels on the floor when you are done showering? It is unkempt and quite distasteful," she would nag.

Sophie and I took every opportunity to poke fun at her.

"Ok, Gen," Sophie would reply in her fake, overly exaggerated, Southern accent. "I will be sure to hang my towel on the rack behind the door. Lord knows we mustn't have any wayward linens on the floor when Colonel Sanders pops over for some sweet tea."

"You know Colonel Sanders is fictional and makes chicken, right?" asked Genevieve, clearly exasperated and unamused by Sophie's pedestrian comment.

"How can he make chicken if he's fictional, Gen?" Sophie asked with feigned curiosity.

I could actually hear Genevieve rolling her eyes next door.

Gen's roommate couldn't have been more different. She was a spunky and quirky little firecracker from Long Island named Isabelle whom everyone just called Bell. She was about 4'10", but she definitely packed a punch. She had the energy and hutzpah of person twice her size. Her dark brown hair was always pulled back into a tight ponytail, and her wardrobe was primarily made up of gym wear or short shorts and tank tops. She consistently had a golden tan (thanks to the tanning salon she frequented in town called "Fake and Bake"), and long acrylic nails painted in glow-in-the-dark hot pink. She also had a mouth like a sailor (as my mother used to say), and she had no trouble whatsoever getting under Gen's skin. She truly had no filter and no shame, and she gave Gen lowkey anxiety.

"Who the fuck cares if we leave our towels on the floor, huh?" she would yell to Genevieve, in her thick New York accent from the other room. "Gimme a break, would ya? You're not my mother. I didn't leave home to go to college to have some new broad over here, busting my balls!"

Again, we could hear Gen rolling her eyes from next door.

It was great fun listening to those two go at it nonstop. "At least we have the bathroom as a buffer," I would admit. "Otherwise, we may need to invest in some earplugs."

"Hell, all we need is a bowl of popcorn and a cocktail," Sophie would retort. "This comedy gold beats anything on TV!"

This statement of Sophie's was particularly poignant, as we didn't have access to any type of television set in our dorm room. We didn't even have a computer. Back in the late 1980s/early 90s, personal computers were pricey and typically only the wealthiest people owned them. Sophie had a word processor that we shared that we used to write our papers. It paled in comparison to an actual PC, but it was definitely better than the janky old typewriter I owned. However, if we wanted to watch a program on TV, we had to walk down the hall to the common room and fight about a dozen other college kids for control of the remote. It usually wasn't pretty. The common room was set squarely between the women's side of the dorm and men's side of the dorm. Inevitably, the women would want to watch some sort of sitcom on TV, while the men usually demanded we watch sports. It often turned into a holy war of the sexes, and Janna, the RA (the resident assistant with an attitude) would march out of her room, snatch the remote control out of someone's hands and yell, "Shut the fuck up! If you can't decide mutually, then none of you get to watch it!" Then, she would promptly do an about face to her room, remote control in tow.

"True, I agree, Soph," I would reply. "Gen and Bell are better than anything on TV anyway!"

***

When we weren't listening to Gen and Bell squabble over every little thing, Sophie and I were busy scouting the dormitory for cute boys. The Big Sur building we lived in was quite large. There were four housing floors with probably 80 rooms per floor. Each room had two occupants. It seemed fairly evenly split between men and women, so we are talking about more than 300 men in this one dorm building. Besides the common rooms on each floor to which every student had access, there was also an enormous 24-hour cafeteria that took up the entire ground floor. Outside, there were a couple of basketball courts, tennis courts, and an Olympic sized swimming pool. All said, there were plenty of spaces to mingle with our fellow dormies.

Soph and I spent countless hours discussing which cute guy was spotted on which part of the property.

"Annie!" Sophie would say in breathless excitement as she came crashing through the dorm room door, "I was just hanging out with Andrea and Carey… you know, the two girls I know from my chemistry lab? Anyway," she continued, "there was a level nine hottie in the common room on the second floor. I have never seen him before! We need to get back there, stat!"

Soph was expert at recon. She had a hot guy radar, and it fired on all cylinders. We also assembled a mental catalogue of all the potential princes throughout Big Sur. We had a ten-point hotness scale, and we usually gave them descriptors that matched either where they lived or where they liked to hang out. For instance, there was "Basketball Court 8.5," "Cafeteria 9," and the coveted "Common Room, third floor, 9.5." Of course, there was also the elusive "Elevator 10" who seemed to elude our GPS. He was a boy we occasionally saw in the elevator or walking across the parking lot. We couldn't seem to figure out which floor he lived on, and we definitely wanted to find out.

As luck would have it, I happened to run into him one morning as I was hustling out the front door of Big Sur, late again, racing to make it on time to my calculus class. As I bounded through the double doors that exited to the sidewalk, I turned the corner swiftly and BANG! I plowed directly into him. On impact, both of us were knocked squarely off our feet. As the initial shock of our collision started to wear off, I stood up and began to gather my belongings that were strewn out of my backpack. I was reluctant to make eye contact with this poor person whom I had just leveled. As I was about to grab the last item, my calculator, I saw a hand reach out and snap it up. I straightened, anticipating that the person I had just run into would be angrily shoving it back into my chest saying something like "Watch where the fuck you're going!" or "What the hell? Slow the fuck down!"

Instead, I looked up to see Elevator 10 kindly, albeit cautiously, handing me back my calculator saying, "Whoa! Easy does it, Barry Allen. Are you ok?"

I about fainted when I saw him. In my mind, I was thinking *Oh my gosh. Thank you so much for being so kind and for not cussing me out right now,* but when I opened my mouth to speak, all that came out was "huh?"

"Barry Allen," he laughed. "You know, the Flash?" He seemed genuinely unscathed by our human fender-bender.

"Oh, right," I replied awkwardly. "Yeah, that really fast, superhero guy." At this point, I wished I was another type of superhero, preferably the type that had the power of invisibility.

"Yeah, the fast guy," he repeated. "Are you all right? Can I get you anything?"

"Uh, yeah," I stammered. "I am fine. Just a little, you know, mortified that I nearly ran right through you." I definitely wished I could disappear in this moment.

"Are you heading to class? You obviously seem like you are in a hurry," he said with a grin. "If not, can I buy you a cup of java at the little coffee café?" he asked with a casual coolness that made me a little dizzy (and not just from the impact moments ago).

"Oh, no," I said. "I was just running out to catch up with my roommate. She left her calculator in our room, and I wanted to get it to her before she left for class. I assume she is long gone now, so I suppose there's no need to rush."

Sure, I missed my calc class, but this was Elevator 10. He was obviously worth it.

***

"Sophie!" I couldn't contain my excitement. "I met him! I met Elevator 10!"

"What!? Where!? How!?" Sophie was just as excited.

I told her the story of my embarrassing run in (literally), as well as the little white lie I told him about where I was heading when I slammed into him. She seemed pleased, and maybe a little honored, that I used her in my clever (albeit fraudulent) excuse.

"What is his name? Where does he live?" she asked.

"His name is Gregory, and he lives on the fourth floor. I guess his roommate ended up freaking out after a week or so into the semester and decided to go back home to Iowa. So, now Gregory has the room all to himself."

Sophie's eyes grew wide, and she blurted out, "Oh my God! This is amazing!"

I gave her the full rundown of our coffee conversation and about all the information I gathered up until that point. He grew up in Idaho, and he was an Earth Sciences major. He said that he wanted to become a geologist and that he particularly enjoyed studying seismic activity. Apparently, this is why he wanted to attend school in California. He was hoping to experience an earthquake. Further, we had several things in common. We were both only children, and we both grew up in a home with two parents and several dogs. We ordered the same coffee (extra hot cinnamon mocha), and we both thought that blueberry scones were entirely overrated. We talked for about an hour in the café before he invited me up to his dorm room. I described the room for Sophie in vivid detail.

"Soph—it was so cool! He pushed the second desk to the same wall as his desk, and then he put the two twin beds together. This gives him twice the storage space as well as a double bed." I was impressed by his ingenuity.

"Oh, wow," she exclaimed. "How lucky that he didn't have to take on another roommate. What exactly happened to the first guy?"

"Oh, I guess he just suffered some sort of culture shock. He was from a small town in the Midwest, and he was a little taken aback by the big city and the enormous campus."

"Yeah," she agreed. "I can see that. It must be strange to come to Southern California from a small Midwestern town. We probably all seem like giant weirdos."

"Yeah, and I guess he was a little apprehensive about the way that Gregory decorated the room."

"Oh!" Sophie squealed. "Do tell!"

"Well, apparently Gregory is very into Bob Marley, reggae music, tossing around his hacky sack, and smoking marijuana. He has gigantic posters of pot leaves on his walls and an impressive collection of pipes on his dresser. I guess his poor roommate decided he was in over his head here."

"Ohhh, ok," Sophie nodded in a knowing way. "So, he's a hippy, huh?"

"Yeah," I conceded, "Maybe. I guess you could say that." I wasn't really sure what a hippy was, but it seemed like an apt label at the time.

"Well, Annie," Sophie inquired in a tone that suggested she was both happy for me and curious to see where this was going, "when are you planning to see your little love hippy again?"

I explained that we had made a plan to hang out in his room again the following day after I got out of class.

"Oh, good," she said with a wink. "Does this mean you will be attending class once again?"

"Very funny," I said with a smirk and an eye roll. "Yes, I am definitely not going to miss another class. I just couldn't pass up that golden opportunity to discover the identity of Elevator 10!"

Sophie understood the logic of my reasoning, and she dropped the subject. "Well, I can't wait to hear how tomorrow goes," she said. As an afterthought, she added, "But tell me this? Did you smoke pot with him?"

"Of course I did, Sophie. What kind of monster would I be if I refused his kind offering?" I feigned outrage at her ridiculous question.

"No wonder you're so giggly, Annabelle. Hide the Doritos!"

We both collapsed into a fit of laughter. She made me promise not to mention any of it to Genevieve, however. "You know she won't approve, Ann," Sophie reasoned.

"And I really don't think you want to hear the lecture, do you?"

I agreed that I undoubtedly did NOT want to hear the lecture, so we decided to keep all of it—Elevator 10, the marijuana, and his living arrangement—as our little secret.

***

The next day came, and I made certain to get up extra early so that I could get properly dressed and primped for the day. While many class sessions were spent in sweats and a t-shirt, with my hair pulled into a messy bun or tucked under a baseball cap, this day I was sure to shower, do my hair and make-up, and pick out a cute outfit. I planned to head straight over to Gregory's room as soon as my mid-morning lecture was over, and I wanted to be all set and ready. As I sat in the classroom, I was eager for the lecture to end so that I could make it back to Big Sur and into what Sophie called the "hippy shack" of Elevator 10. I remember sitting through my World Literature class just watching the clock tick along with absolutely zero urgency. While my professor lectured about one of my favorite novels, Gabriel Garcia Márquez' *One Hundred Years of Solitude,* I couldn't help but become distracted, thinking about what my afternoon would be like with Gregory. While taking notes on the multi-generational narrative of the Buendia family, I found myself drawing little hearts with E-10 inside of them. If I were attempting to be more accurate, I should have drawn little pot leaves with E-10 inside of them.

Nonetheless, I was eager to jet out of class and head back to BS for what I imagined would be a rousing afternoon.

As soon as I entered the building, I went straight to the elevator, backpack in tow, and hit the button for the fourth floor. Luckily, the elevator was in operation this afternoon, and I didn't have to brave the stairs. I considered whether or not I should head up to my room on the fifth floor first so that I could drop off my backpack. In the end, I decided that I didn't want to spend the extra 5-10 minutes it would take to go the extra floor. Even though I wanted to give myself one quick glance over to see if I needed to reapply lipstick or powder my nose, I figured I could ask to use his restroom when I got to Gregory's room. Besides, I was afraid that Gen may be in our room, and I didn't want to explain where I was going. She fancied herself the mother hen of our suite, and she was always poking her nose into our business. The last thing I needed was an inquisition into the life and times of Elevator 10. Gen could be quite judgy, especially about boys. If she knew about Gregory's marijuana-themed bachelor pad, I would never hear the end of it.

I knocked on Gregory's door, jittery with excitement at seeing Elevator 10 again. However, nothing happened. I waited maybe 30 seconds, and I knocked again, this time with a little more gusto. Still nothing. I started retracing the steps of our conversation in my mind. *We did say today, right?* I told him I would be over around noon. I looked at my pink and purple Swatch watch. It was 12:15 p.m. *Was he still in class? Maybe I should wait for a few minutes.* I knocked one more time for good measure, but he never opened the door. Disappointed, I figured that I just simply misunderstood the plan. Perhaps we were supposed to meet later or even the following day. I decided to write him a little note and slip it under the door. I grabbed a piece of notebook paper from my backpack (suddenly pleased that I decided to keep it after all), and I contemplated what to write. I definitely didn't want to seem too eager, but I also didn't want to appear too aloof. I decided to just play it cool and casual. I wrote, "Hey, Gregory. I just stopped by to hang out. Looks like I missed you. Feel free to swing by my room if you want. I am in room 524. XO, Annie." I wasn't sure if the "XO" was too much, but I figured it was probably fine. It was flirty, right? As I kneeled down to slip the paper under the door, Gregory suddenly opened it.

In my surprise, I jumped back, nearly falling on my rear end.

"Oh!" he said, "there you are!" he seemed genuinely pleased to see me.

"Oh, hey," I replied, a little confused by what was happening and embarrassed that I was still there after basically pounding on the door for several minutes. "I didn't think you were home. I was just going to leave you a note," I said, hoping to imply that the reason I was there for so long was that I had to spend time finding some paper and writing the message.

As I spoke, I looked past him into his room. It was like looking into a foggy marsh. The only light that shone was the dim glow of the record player dials, and the minimal light that came in from between the horizontal blinds that covered his one small window. The smell of pot smoke was thick and pervasive to say the least.

He gently pulled me in to his room, saying "better come in quick. I don't want the RA to get a whiff. He will be down here in a minute harshing our buzz."

I entered the room, immediately dizzy from the contact high I was surely experiencing. I sat down on his bed, and I asked him why he didn't answer the door right away. I suspected he was in the bathroom or something, but he just said, "Oh, yeah. I heard a knock, but I wasn't sure where it was coming from. I thought maybe it was outside. I looked out the window, but I didn't see anything. Then, I heard it again. This time I thought maybe it was inside my chest. I started to wonder if I could hear my heart beating. But then, after a while, I remembered that it might be my door. And I remembered you might be coming over, so I answered the door, and there you were." He acted as though this were a perfectly normal response. Turns out, Gregory was just really, *really* high.

Although I had some fun times in his hippy shack, I wish I could say that my relationship with Gregory blossomed into a love story for the ages. Sadly, however, this was not the case. Aside from our first chance encounter that brought us to the little coffee café outside of Big Sur, we never left his dorm room again. Literally. Aside from going to his classes very occasionally, all Gregory wanted to do was smoke weed, listen to reggae music, and "chill." "Chilling" was all fine, well, and good... but it did get old rather quickly. I just couldn't get high every day like that. For me, it was a once in a blue moon sort of activity; for Gregory, it was a way of life. Before too long, I stopped meeting Gregory in his room altogether. To be honest, I'm not certain if he even noticed I wasn't there. By the end of our freshman year, I heard through the grapevine that Gregory failed all of his classes and went back home to Idaho. I often wonder what became of him. I will always remember him as Elevator 10: a stone-cold hottie, though empty inside (save for a shit ton of pot smoke).

As our freshman year ended, Sophie and I said our goodbyes to Big Sur, and to our dormies, and we made our way back to our parents' homes for the summer. It was a bittersweet moment when we packed up our belongings and exited BS for the last time. I had a lot of fun, and I felt like I had accomplished a lot in that year, but I certainly didn't complete my prime directive. I was no closer to finding my prince charming than I had been when I graduated from high school. However, I had three more years to go, and I felt excited and optimistic about my chances. Little did I know, sophomore year would certainly deliver.

Chapter 4: Nash

After the chaotic yet exciting year of dorm life, our summer was rather dull. Sophie and I said we would stay in contact with Genevieve and Isabelle, but once we went our separate ways, we completely lost touch. Our summer was mainly spent catching up with our old high school friends who went to different universities. We compared notes and debated which school had the best parties and which school had the worst cafeterias. We swapped stories about our hook ups, one-night stands, and relationships. I was a little embarrassed to admit that the only real action I saw my freshman year involved Elevator 10. Some of my old classmates actually came home with promise rings. In any event, like Sophie reminded me, freshman year was just the warmup drill. We had three prime years of play time ahead of us. While we had a decent time hanging out back at home, we couldn't help but feel like we were going backwards. All we wanted to do was get back to school and begin our second year of college.

The summer finally came to an end, and Sophie and I were thrilled to be heading back to our university. The best news of all? Our parents relented and allowed us to lease an off-campus apartment. We talked them into it by reasoning that since they wouldn't have to pay for the meal plan required by the dorms, it would actually be a wash. We promised that we would keep a modest grocery bill and not spend any more money than we needed. I even vowed to get a job at a restaurant so that I could possibly bring home extra food at the end of my shifts. From what I knew about restaurant life from spending time at Sophie's house, there was always extra food that could be taken home after closing. If I am being honest, Sophie concocted the whole idea about the off-campus apartment. She crafted the case and then expertly persuaded them to see the logic in her argument. She sincerely was a lawyer in the making. I just went along with it, dropping in an occasional *Yeah! What she said!* for good measure.

As we were handed the keys to our very own apartment, we were ecstatic and felt like we had finally landed a leading role in our own lives. We were officially women now. We were sophomores in college, and we were out on our own. It was a tiny apartment… just one bedroom and one bathroom, probably 800 square feet… but it was ours. We were already used to sharing close quarters, though, so this place seemed enormous. Instead of sharing the bathroom with a couple of other women, it was just the two of us. And, we also had a small living room (complete with a TV), and a small kitchen. Who could ask for anything more?

We had so much fun decorating this apartment. We were on a very tight budget, obviously, so our décor mostly consisted of treasures found at a local thrift shop, trinkets we brought from home, and unframed posters. Sophie's favorite piece that we acquired was a purple lava lamp that she called Grimace (named after the famous, bulbous McDonaldland character). It sat atop our avocado green, thrift store, chest of drawers, alongside an Alf stuffed animal that we had received as a gag gift from Bell. That Alf doll always made us laugh. My favorite piece of apartment accoutrement was the poster of Michael Schoeffling that we had hanging in the bathroom. Michael Schoeffling played the gorgeous Jake Ryan in the 1984 classic rom com *16 Candles*. Sophie and I were obsessed with this film, and we thought Jake Ryan was as close to perfection as any fictional teenaged boy could be. We had a friend from Big Sur who worked at the local movie theater. She snagged a copy of the poster from their archives and gave it to us as a housewarming gift. We couldn't have been more excited.

In addition to living in our very own apartment and finally laying claim to our adulthood, sophomore year was also the year that I met my first *real* college boyfriend. I say *real* college boyfriend because Gregory doesn't really count. Can you actually be in a relationship with a guy who never takes you on a date… never even leaves the dorm room? Seems counter-intuitive to me. No, Gregory was more of an acquaintance or even a crush than a boyfriend. Therefore, my *real* boyfriend arrived my second year of college, and his name was Nash. His name was actually Owen Nash, but he said Owen was a "dorky" name, so he exclusively went by his last name. Besides, he was a football player, so he was used to being called by his last name anyway. I laughed when I first met him, as his real name always reminded me of an off-beat film from the 1980s called *Throw Momma from the Train* starring Billy Crystal and Danny DeVito. There's a line from the film when Momma (played by the brilliant Anne Ramsey) suddenly comes upon a young man whom she finds in her home named Larry (played by the incomparable Billy Crystal). She demands, "Who the hell are you?" Crystal replies, wide-eyed "I'm Owen's friend." Ramsey doesn't skip a beat and retorts, "Owen doesn't have a friend... he's fat and he's stupid." I still chuckle to this day when I think about Owen Nash.

Unlike the arguably unattractive Owen from the 1980s film, Nash was truly a spectacular physical specimen. What I mean to say is, he was outright gorgeous. He looked like a Greek God... if Greek Gods were half African American and half German. He had light brown skin and intense, green-blue eyes. He wore his hair in short dreadlocks, and constantly had a smile on his beautifully chiseled face.

"Why are you always smiling?" I once asked him.

"I always smile when I am around you," he lovingly replied.

Wow. That saccharine bullshit was music to my 19-year-old ears.

I met Nash while waiting in line at the college bookstore. I was there to purchase a psychology textbook and some new highlighters, and the guy in line in front of me struck up a conversation. He was a good conversationalist, and I found myself laughing at his jokes and feeling mesmerized by his intense eyes. After the 30-minute bookstore wait, he walked me all the way back to my apartment, and we stood in the doorway talking for almost another half-hour. The time just flew by as we chatted about our favorite classes, our favorite professors, and the best places to buy snacks on campus. I asked him if he wanted to come in and continue our chat, but he said he had to run because he couldn't be late for practice.

"Coach will make us all do 50 up downs if we are late," he told me. I had no idea what that was, but from the tone in his voice, it sounded dreadful. "But can I see you on Sunday?" he asked.

My head swirled for a moment, and I responded with an enthusiastic, "Absolutely!" I sort of regretted the over-eager tone in my voice, but it was too late. I had said it, and there was no taking it back now. Nash didn't miss a beat to say "Awesome," and he gave me a quick peck on the cheek and ran off toward the stadium. The rest, as they say, was history. Nash and I became inseparable after that day.

I thought I had found my Prince Charming for sure. I went home a few weeks after we began dating, and I told my parents all about him. If my mother was more than happy with this flourishing relationship, my father was over the moon. Nash was a star football player at our division 1 university. He was on television every Saturday. The bragging rights were epic.

"He is quite a catch, Annabelle. I have a really good feeling about this one. But, honestly, dear… Are you making sure to eat well and exercise? Nash clearly takes his physical fitness seriously, and he most definitely wants a woman who is equally fit. I noticed you are getting a little soft in the midsection, sweetie. Have you been eating too much food in that university cafeteria? You know they use substandard ingredients, and those tasty, snack foods often include empty calories. Try to eat more fruits and vegetables. Also, be sure to do some sit-ups. Oh, and it wouldn't hurt to fast for a day every other week or so."

Although she meant well, turns out my mother was fat shaming me before fat shaming was even a thing.

"Yes, Mother. I am doing my best. I am taking an aerobics class at school, and I am counting my calories. I rarely eat pre-packaged snack foods, and I only drink Diet Coke, never the real thing. I can't seem to maintain a completely flat stomach though. I am not sure why." *It could be the 25 cent beers we hammer every Thursday night at the local hangout that doesn't card college students,* I thought (but didn't dare say out loud).

My mother took every opportunity to remind me that smart women go to college to earn their "MRS" degrees. At the time, I thought she may be right because Nash was the complete package. He was smart, athletic, and handsome. Although he was there at this D1 football school on an athletic scholarship, he was also a physics major with a 3.5 GPA. So, really, he was no dummy. He did, however, have one teeny, tiny problem that ended up being what one might call a *deal-breaker...* turns out he was also a sexual predator. Oops.

We dated for maybe three or four months, and, in that time, he played the perfect gentleman. He scoffed at the other players on his team who were obviously sleeping around recklessly, saying things like: "They just don't understand what we have. Once you find the one you are meant to be with, you don't need anyone else." So, yeah, he was charming and chivalrous at first. He definitely was.

I even brought Nash home with me one weekend. If I thought my mother rolled out the red carpet for Oz when I was in high school, the level of preparations she made for Nash were off the charts. She did reconnaissance for weeks.

"What are his favorite foods, Annabelle," she would ask, desperate to ensure that the cupboards were stocked with all of his preferences.

"We will only be there for two days, Mom. You don't need to completely re-do the kitchen pantry!"

Unfazed, she replied "Annabelle, he will be our guest. The least I can do is have some creature comforts prepared for him. Besides, I suspect he may be on a strict diet due to his exceptional physical prowess."

When we arrived on Saturday afternoon, my mother was rushing around the house, tidying up, and making sure everything was just so. My dad greeted us at the door, and within seconds, he presented Nash with an 8x10 glossy of the football team and asked him to autograph it. I about died of embarrassment. Fortunately, he was a good sport, and he signed it: "Nash # 21"

Everything went perfectly well that weekend, and my parents certainly approved of him. Hell, they more than approved. They borderline worshipped him.

Nash played right into their hands. He was sure to compliment my mother on her exceptional cooking, and he asked my father if he played any ball in school. Nash said he could just tell that my father had a "natural gift" for athleticism. Nash also spoke extremely lovingly to me and about me. He told my parents I was the best thing about college, even better than winning that bowl game last season. My parents took the bait: hook, line, and sinker.

Despite the obvious embellishment on his part, I did believe that he was falling for me. And how did I feel? I was sincerely smitten. What could be better than a hot, handsome, hunk of a man who has the admiration and ultimate approval of my parents? I felt like I hit the jackpot.

Unfortunately, all of this splendor came crashing down one night in early May, right before we left for summer break. I was living in our one-bedroom apartment with Soph, but she had gone out of town for the weekend to visit one of her cousins who was going to school back East. Nash knew we would have the apartment to ourselves, so he asked if he could sleep over. Up to this point, I had never spent the entire night with him. He roomed with several guys from the football team, and I had this one-bedroom place with Sophie. My parents made sure we slept in different rooms at their house, and honestly, that was fine. I would have felt extremely uncomfortable getting intimate with Nash in my childhood home with my parents mere steps away. Therefore, when this opportunity presented itself, I was eager to make it happen.

I remember it like it was yesterday. We had just come in from seeing a romantic comedy at the local theater. We laughed all the way home as we recounted the unrealistic plot, and we settled into an easy, casual stride. As we entered my apartment, I dropped my purse in the living room and went to freshen up in the restroom. When I came back out, I saw that Nash had made his way into my bedroom. I turned the corner, and I was confronted with a startling sight. Nash was laying squarely on my bed, completely naked. Now, this was not the first time I had seen him nude, but this was the first time he stripped down so quickly, so brazenly. We usually started out by kissing and groping, and then one thing would naturally lead to another. I was a little taken aback by seeing him just spread out on my bed, but I wouldn't say that I was upset. We had been sexually active for at least a couple of weeks now, and I definitely wanted it to continue.

"Come lay down with me, Baby," he said with a tone of urgency.

I started crossing the room, but he quickly interrupted, "but take off your clothes first. Do it slowly. I want to watch."

I was a little uncomfortable with stripping down right there in the middle of my bedroom, with him watching me no less, but I figured this is what adults do. They strip down naked, slowly, in front of each other. I assumed he was just trying to take advantage of this rare opportunity to have the apartment all to ourselves, so I did my best to calm my nerves and just go with the flow.

As I awkwardly undressed, he began to masturbate. Aside from a creepy porno a babysitter once made me watch when I was around 10 or 11 years old (that's another story), this was the first time I had actually seen a grown man masturbate. It sort of excited me, I guess, but it sort of scared me too. It was one of those situations where I didn't want to look but I couldn't look away. I suddenly felt very cold.

I made the snap decision to just undress as quickly as possible (despite his request to do it slowly) because I was embarrassed and simply wanted it over. I suddenly felt like an awkward teenager trying to play stripper, and it made me very uncomfortable. I dropped the final piece of clothing, my undies, onto the floor, and I jumped into bed with him.

He immediately slid on top of me, and I started to calm down a bit, as this was a position I was more familiar with. However, instead of kissing me or even sliding himself into me as he had several times before, he decided to continue masturbating while sitting on top of me. He pulled my arms down and straddled my chest, his knees pressing into my arms, trapping them down. His penis was inches from my face, and I was trapped beneath the weight of him. I could hardly breathe.

I began to mildly protest: "Nash! What are you doing? This is kinda weird."

"It's ok, Baby. Trust me. You'll like it" he said, obviously not intending to stop.

Now my heart rate started to accelerate. I was squirming and attempting to free myself, but I was unable. He was too big and too strong. I started to get visibly upset. "Nash! Stop it! I'm not playing. I can't breathe! Get off of me!"

My protests seemed to make him more excited, as he started jerking off harder and faster. "Yeah, Annie. Tell me to stop!" he said, with breathless excitement.

This is when it hit me. *Oh my God. He is assaulting me, and he is actually getting off on it.*

"Please, Nash!" I begged. "Please get off of me. I don't like this. I really don't. You are hurting me! I can't breathe. I want you off of me NOW!" I tried to scream, but the sheer weight of him was squeezing my body to the point where I felt like I could pass out from asphyxiation at any moment.

As my protest fell on deaf ears, I realized that his size and strength were too much for me to fight. I decided to just lay still, try to stop crying so I could actually get oxygen to flow in and out of my lungs, and attempt to fight back the tears that were now silently falling down my face.

After what felt like a lifetime (but was probably only about 3 or 4 minutes), he came. Yes, he ejaculated onto my face while he said these elegant words to me in this order: "Take. My. Jizz." Wow, poetry.

When he finally slumped off of me, pleased with what he had wrought, I jumped to my feet, grabbed a blanket, and ran to my next-door neighbor's apartment, screaming bloody murder. Nash was in a state of shock, it appeared, seemingly wondering what the hell was wrong.

I pounded on my neighbor's door, and he finally opened it up to see me, cloaked in a blanket, with a smear of tears, mascara, snot, and semen across my face. I yelled for him to call 9-1-1 and that I had been raped. Nash heard this exchange and decided he had better leave. So as quickly as he came (ugh), he left. He bailed out of my apartment, clothes in tow, and sped off in his piece of shit, 1982 Honda Civic.

The cops finally arrived, and I went through the entire harrowing encounter while my neighbor, whom I barely knew, sat there looking pekid, though he was trying, I think, to be supportive.

"So, did you know the suspect?" the first cop asked me.

"Yeah, I know him. We are, or *were,* dating," I replied, emphasizing the "were."

"Hmmmm, I see," the other cop said as he gave his partner a knowing smirk.

"Were you engaged in an *intimate* relationship with this gentleman?" he asked.

Gentleman? I thought. *Did I not just tell you he is a predator?* "Um, if are you asking me if we had slept together before, then the answer is yes, but..." he didn't let me finish.

"Uh huh, I see," he interrupted.

These two bozos went on to ask me very specific questions, pausing for lurid details, in a way that at the time felt strange but not altogether inappropriate. Looking back on it, I think they were titillated by the exchange.

"So, how much ejaculate would you estimate he expelled?" one of the policemen asked, as if he were more impressed than curious.

"How much?" I asked... "I don't know! A lot! Too much!" I wasn't sure why that mattered.

Finally, after nearly an hour of questioning and vivid detail-telling, they recommended that I stop seeing him if I was not into "that sort of thing."

"What!?" I was outraged. "*Into* that sort of thing?" I repeated. "Who would be into sexual, fucking, assault!?"

"Now, now, honey. Don't get so upset. I would hardly call it an assault. It *certainly* wasn't rape. He didn't even penetrate you." He looked at his partner who was shaking his head in affirmation, "This is just another classic case of miscommunication."

"Are you fucking kidding me? There was NO communication. I told you that. I asked him to get off of me and he didn't!" I could hardly believe what I was hearing.

"Easy, easy, little lady. There's no need to shout. We are here trying to help you," the one cop said while his dumbass partner nodded. They both had looks on their faces that suggested something to the effect of "*We got a live one here. No wonder the poor boy was confused...*"

"It doesn't feel like you are trying to help me at all," I said through gritted teeth. "In fact, it feels like you are trying to NOT help me. I told you that I was assaulted, and you are refusing to do a goddamn thing about it. Will you at least file a report?" I demanded.

"Sweetie," the one cop said with a tone that suggested he was speaking to a child who was throwing a temper tantrum on the floor, "if we filed a report every time a girl decided she no longer liked having sex with her boyfriend, we wouldn't have any time left to fight real crime."

Yeah. He said those words to me.

So, there it was. The verdict had been made. Tweedledee and/or Tweedle-fucking-dum made one more patronizing comment to my neighbor about helping me calm down because I was "hysterical," and they were off. Just like that, I was denigrated to a weepy, frenzied, co-ed with another bullshit claim of rape. *Poor bastard,* they probably thought to themselves, as they strolled back to their patrol car. *And they wonder why guys today are reluctant to commit. They have to put up with bat-shit crazy gals like that.*

Luckily for me, I never saw Nash again. Well, that's not entirely true. I did see him, one time, maybe a week or two after the fateful incident. He was walking across the quad as Sophie and I made our way to our history class to take our final exam. Our eyes met, briefly, and I saw something in them that made me smile. It was a look I had never observed in his eyes before. It wasn't a look of shame or regret, but it was something just as satisfying to me. It was a look of something akin to fear. He quickly put his head down and raced in the opposite direction.

Huh, I thought. *How odd.* If only he knew that the cops couldn't care less about my claim. Well, I certainly wasn't going to be the one to tell him. I rather enjoyed the thought of him living in fear of repercussions that ultimately would never come. I fantasized about him dangling like a powerless fish caught helpless on a line, or like a sly, cunning fox caught in a camouflaged snare… or like a predatory football player caught with his pants down and his man-parts set in the crosshairs of a firearm scope. Ok, maybe that last part was a bit much, but a fantasy is a fantasy.

"You'd better fucking run!" Sophie yelled at him for good measure. We laughed when we saw him scurrying away. "Pathetic rat," she said to me, as he quickly disappeared behind the Humanities building, tail between his legs.

Good riddance, I thought to myself. *I hope you get tackled ruthlessly at your next game. Then, you can see how it feels to be trapped, wind knocked out of you, naked and afraid, begging for mercy.* Ok, he obviously wouldn't be naked, but wouldn't it be amazing if he were.

Chapter 5: Quinton

A few weeks after my harrowing experience with Nash took place, I went home for the summer. Going home was always a little weird. To put it mildly, I hated it. It was like I was living in two distinct and disparate worlds. Away at college, living with Sophie, I was an adult, a mature woman. I was in charge of my life, and I made my own choices (for better or for worse). I came and went as I pleased, and I answered to no one. At home, I was a child. What's more, I was the only child of two loving but often overbearing parents who seemed oblivious to the fact that just mere weeks prior, I was living my life in any way that I desired. At home, I was faced with curfews, rules, and an utter lack of privacy. To make matters worse, Sophie wasn't around much that summer. She was selected for a very prestigious internship in Washington DC, and it took her to the East Coast for almost two months. So, not only was I subjected to my parents treating me like a helpless adolescent, I didn't even have Sophie or Sophie's house as a refuge.

Despite the less-than-optimal circumstances, I tried to make the most of it. I tried to remind myself that it was good to spend some quality time with my mom and dad. I knew my parents loved having me home, and I felt slightly guilty every time I bemoaned yet another family dinner around the three-person dinner table. I also knew it was an especially difficult summer, as my mom had just lost both of my namesake's pups, Starbelle and Cooper, that spring. They had lived a very long life, but their bodies no longer worked properly. She had to make the heart-breaking decision to put them down. I wondered if their collars would also adorn a framed portrait of them, but I didn't observe any pictures on the wall. In many ways, I was happy to be there to provide my mother with some emotional support, or at least a distraction from her significant loss. Certainly, it was nice to return the favor for once. She was always there for me when I needed her, so it was the least I could do to be there for her in her time of sorrow. Secretly, however, I was counting down the days until I could return to my college apartment and what I considered to be my *real* life.

What was even worse than not having Sophie around to occupy my time, was the fact that I was forced to listen to my parents' relentless admonishment about how I let Nash slip through my fingers. I told them it was an amicable and mutual decision to break up. Not only did I not want to worry them with the details of their daughter's sexual assault, I also didn't necessarily want to admit to them that I was sexually active. While I am not sure it would have been an absolute shock, I do know they would feel compelled to scold me for having sex outside of marriage and insist on taking me to the doctor to receive a prescription for birth control pills. For one thing, that discussion would be awkward and humiliating at best. For another thing, I was already on birth control (thanks to the health center on campus that offered free birth control pills to students), and that was yet another secret I wasn't ready to reveal. Consequently, it seemed best to simply lie and tell them that Nash and I mutually decided to go our separate ways. It felt like the easiest and, honestly, kindest thing to do. My parents didn't seem to buy it, however. Dad was forlorn, his hopes for a famous son-in-law football player dashed; Mom gave me wicked side-eye and clearly suspected I wasn't keeping up adequately with my diet and fitness routine. Either way, the summer was a long and arduous one.

Finally, after two months of looking through photo albums of the now-dead dogs and accompanying Mom to her church group outings, the day in mid-August finally came, and I was ready to head back to university. Sophie had returned from DC a couple of weeks before, and we were excited to get back to our *real* lives at school. We crammed in all of the clothing we had brought home and acquired over the summer into our cars, and we caravanned back to our college apartment. We had been subletting it to some grad students who were there for a fellowship over the summer. We assumed that they would take good care of the place in our absence, and our suspicions were accurate. We walked into the apartment and, frankly, it looked better than when we left it in May.

School started as it usually did, and Sophie and I worked our magic to the best of our ability to schedule our classes in sync. Although we were different majors and couldn't take all of the same classes, we did our best to take our general education courses together and to schedule our classes at the same basic times each day. Although it was never an exact match, we did fairly well. We also vowed to start this school year with a renewed commitment to find our Prince Charmings. As luck would have it, Sophie and I took the same anthropology course and were assigned to the same discussion section taught by a grad school teaching assistant (TA) by the name of William. We knew Will from the restaurant where I worked; he was a regular there, and he dated my manager off and on. Will was a pretty cool guy for a TA (trust me, some of them were insufferable blowhards), and he often held study sessions and social outings outside of class. It was at one of these social sessions that I met the young man I would date next: Quinton.

After suffering the humiliation and fear surrounding my disturbing sexual relationship with Nash, I opted to go in a completely different direction. Enter: Quinton. Quinton was a darling young man. He really was. He was a double major, philosophy and political science. He liked to read... and talk... and write... and talk. He was also taking the same anthropology lecture that Sophie and I were in, so we had that in common. After my traumatic experience with Nash, I wasn't interested in an aggressive or even assertive male partner. Truly, I rebounded into a very different kind of relationship. I was a junior in college now, and I realized that I needed--no! I deserved!--a mature, refined man. Quinton, as it were, fit the bill perfectly.

It was at one of these extracurricular social outings that Sophie and I spotted him. To say that Quinton was *sweet* would be a vast understatement. He was a gentle snowflake of a man. Unlike the strapping physique of Nash, the football god, Quinton was a slight, spindly young fellow. He wore leather bracelets and tied his stringy, mid-length hair into a tidy bun (before the man-bun was even a thing.). I actually made the first move on Quinton that fall. I went up to him at one of our study sessions, and I said, "Hi! I am Annie. Do you want to get a cup of coffee and study for the midterm together?" He initially looked a bit stunned at my forward approach, but he quickly settled into a position of appreciation. He later told me that he had never had a woman approach him and ask him out like that. I think he felt both complimented and relieved.

My relationship with Quinton evolved quickly. I found that I was able to set the pace, and, apparently, I figured the pace should be "full steam ahead." Sophie was pleased that I had moved past the ugliness of Nash, but I wouldn't say she was a superfan of Quinton. She didn't hold anything against him, per se, but she would often use this word to describe him: meh.

"I mean, he's *fine,* Annie," she would say, "but I guess I just see you with someone with a little more pizzaz… a bit more *je ne sais quoi.*"

"Yeah," I would concede, "I can see what you mean. But honestly, Soph," I would retort, "at least he is a decent guy. He treats me with respect and doesn't, ya know, pin me down for shits and giggles."

"True," Sophie agreed, "but, let's face it, Ann. He couldn't pin you down, even if he tried."

"Ok," I would acknowledge. "Fair statement."

Unlike Nash, or Oz, or really any guy I had ever dated or even known, Quinton was truly comfortable with all things home related. He actually took the time to iron his button-up Oxford shirts, and he wore them proudly with his earth-toned corduroy pants and loafers. Yes, he owned an iron and an ironing board, and he knew how to use them.

"You've hit the jackpot!" my mother would cry, when we spoke about Quinton's penchant for domestic life.

Quinton would sometimes mildly try to coax me into ironing my own clothes as well. I occasionally took the bait (mostly because I could tell that he was embarrassed by my apparently disheveled attire), but I secretly loathed doing it. I vowed to avoid buying garments that required ironing in the future and tried to run my clothes through the dryer before seeing him in a last-ditch effort to minimize any wrinkles. Unlike Quinton, however, there was definitely no starch in my laundry cabinet.

"Annabelle!" my mother would chide, "Would it kill you to take an interest in domestic matters? How embarrassed you must be that your darling boyfriend is more adept in homemaking than you are!"

I couldn't roll my eyes any harder if I tried.

Although I didn't mind some of the perks of Quinton's skills in the home, actual dates with him could be somewhat daunting. I remember visiting an art gallery with Quinton one time. Although I was an English major, I had taken a few art history courses, and I certainly enjoyed viewing the pieces. I would never profess to be any sort of expert in the field, but I felt like I could view the artwork with at least a semblance of understanding, prior knowledge, and critical thinking. Quinton, however, considered himself to be the Frank O'Hara of art criticism. He would attempt to gather crowds to profess the symbolism of the red dot in the foreground or the uneven patterns of flowers in the background.

"Now what we have here is the artist screaming for liberation in a vacuum of poignancy and nostalgia," I could hear him tell the partially rapt audience of Midwestern tourists.

I suppose this behavior wouldn't be annoying if I thought for a moment he knew what the hell he was talking about. For Quinton, he seemed to simply talk for the joy of talking… the sheer ecstasy of hearing his own voice slip through his lips. His prose was insufferable, and his reasoning was often circular. Honestly, he was a bit of a windbag.

Although Quinton could definitely be described as "meek," he was also arguably (though subtly) arrogant too. He believed he was smarter than the average person, and he took great pride in his ability to speak three languages: English, French and Italian. Though, looking back, who knows if this was legit. I only had a handle on one, English, so he could have been bullshitting me about the other two the entire time. I suppose I will never know. It was also the way that he communicated his vast linguistic knowledge that rubbed me the wrong way. He seized any opportunity to show off his trilingual abilities. I remember one time, we were walking along the sidewalk in a touristy area that housed a bunch of quaint shops and restaurants. He overheard a couple speaking in what I can only assume was Italian (based on my very limited knowledge which was composed exclusively from hearing Sophie's extended family yell at each other at holiday parties), and he sauntered over to them post haste. He butted right into their conversation and started practicing his Italian with them. I have absolutely no idea what he said, but the couple looked more confused than engaged. I will never know if the confusion was based on the fact that Quinton spoke in broken (or even obliterated) Italian or if they were simply taken aback that this stranger decided to insert himself, inelegantly, into their otherwise private conversation. Either way, it clearly was not what one might consider a pleasant interaction.

"Hmph," Quinton huffed as he left the couple and returned to my side. "And they say Americans are rude!"

I am not sure what the couple said to Quinton, but apparently, he didn't appreciate it. Whatever it was, I can't say that I blamed them.

Quinton also enjoyed enlightening me on the deep and subversive messages of various works of literature. Despite the fact that I was the English major and should have been considered the resident authority on the matter, Quinton regularly waxed poetic about the hidden meaning of whatever piece of poetry or prose that he read.

"I'm telling you, Annie, Allen Ginsberg knew exactly who killed JFK! It is all there in *Howl,*" he would argue.

He also wrote his own creative pieces and would come home enraged when, once again, his poem was rejected by the likes of *The New Yorker* or the *Atlantic Monthly.*

"They wouldn't know good poetry, Annie, if it kissed them on the lips," he would groan.

Sure, Quinton, The New Yorker *just doesn't seem to have its finger on the pulse of talent,* I would think to myself.

For fun, Quinton would have a few friends over to his apartment, decorated like a page out of a *Good Housekeeping* magazine of course, for wine and cheese parties. He would line up the cheeses on a little wooden platter, and he would make sweeping declarations about which supermarket cheese paired perfectly with which grocery store wine. My

God, who was he kidding? He worked as a sandwich-maker at the deli on campus. His hands smelled like mustard and broken dreams. He barely made enough money to buy his books each semester, but he fancied himself a wine and cheese connoisseur.

Even our friends became annoyed at his boastful antics. Sure, they liked the free wine and fromage, but that free wine and cheese wasn't free at all; it came at a steep price. That price was humoring Quinton and listening, *once again*, to his theories about emergent evolution. Fine, that may be all well and good to discuss with one's philosophy professor, but trust me, the average college kid doesn't give a shit about that on a Saturday night.

Sex with Quinton was also lack-luster to say the least. After Nash, I obviously was not interested in jumping into a relationship with an aggressive sexual partner. However, I went in the complete opposite direction. Quinton enjoyed kissing and hugging and caressing one another. Yes, this was all delightful--at first--but it became rather stale rather quickly. He never wanted to rush... always insisted we take our time. Even when I was dead tired after working a late shift at the restaurant (I worked as a waitress at a fine-dining establishment in town called *Seaside*), he would insist on a couple's bubble bath and sensual massage. If this seemingly never-ending foreplay ever actually ended in coitus, it was quite uninspiring. It would involve a few tender thrusts, a breathless "*Oh, God!*" and a few minutes of gentle weeping. Yes, Quinton cried after sex. It oddly made *me* feel like a sexual predator, but they were "tears of joy" he would assert.

"Tears," he once told me, "are the spiritual equivalent of my semen."

Yep, put that one on a Hallmark card.

Quinton said he was bursting with love for me... from both ends of his physical body. Apparently, tears were the literal manifestation of his deep affection. Wow. Really? From where I was sitting, he looked like a scared, little boy who lost his puppy. From my perspective, this weepy display did not incite passion, and it was certainly not sexy.

Surprisingly, even though I was somewhat repulsed by his tender affect, we actually had a decent relationship. We got along fairly well, and we made some fun memories. I secretly loved the fact that he took great pride in his cooking abilities, as it meant I was treated to a delicious home-cooked meal several nights a week. After working in a restaurant, the last thing I wanted was take-out. Well, that's the second to last thing I wanted. The very last thing I wanted was to cook for myself. So, this arrangement suited me, even if I did have to endure the occasional bubble bath and interminable make-out session.

Sophie used to tease me mercilessly about him. She would ask how my man-baby was doing and then taunt me by singing the childhood song: *Annie and Quinton, sitting in a tree. K-I-S-S-I-N-G.* When I would leave the apartment to head over to his house, she would hand me a box of tissues, wink, and say "for after." I would roll my eyes and say, "very funny, Soph," but inside I would be laughing raucously. She definitely wasn't wrong.

Although we got along reasonably well, there were times when Quinton and I would have a disagreement. When he and I would quarrel, it would inevitably end in an apology letter (I can only assume that's what it was) written by him. This letter would be a hand-written poem or prose, penned in French, and signed with some awkwardly constructed English salutation like "Ever yours" or "Faithfully thine" or some other weird, old-timey phrase. At first, I thought it was a lovely, romantic gesture. Over time, it became an unbearable nuisance. To be honest, I never took the time to get the letters translated, so perhaps they were actually fuck-you letters. Or maybe they were complete gibberish. Maybe the joke was on me. Nonetheless, his gentle-nature and annoying French notes started wearing very thin on me in time.

Although there were plenty of pieces of evidence that suggested that this relationship would not, in fact, go the distance, the final nail in the coffin of our relationship was the way that he ate his cereal. I know, call me shallow. I get it. But I honestly just couldn't take it. Despite his alleged proclivity for fine dining, he ate cereal every single day, and not exclusively for breakfast. Although this fact in and of itself was not completely intolerable, the way that he held the bowl was, in my earnest opinion, a deal-breaker. He cupped the bowl in one up-turned palm and fed the cereal into his mouth with the spoon he gingerly held in his other hand. Even when there was a table near-by, Quinton would cup that bowl as gently as if he were cupping his own balls, and daintily spoon the cereal into his tiny, birdlike mouth. It was too much to witness. I simply knew I had to get out.

Sure, Mother was disappointed. "He will be *the one who got away,* Annie!" she would admonish me. Inside, I would think *No, Mom. I seriously don't think so. Let him go.*

Yet, at this point, I was more than halfway through my college experience, and I still hadn't found *Mr. Right.*

"What are you going to do?" she'd exclaim.

But who was she kidding? There was no way I could marry this guy. By the end of our six-month relationship, I couldn't even stand to hear him speak. Every word that came out of his manicured mouth sounded like defeat.

Luckily, that summer I decided to take the big leap. I begged my parents to allow me to stay in our apartment with Sophie instead of going home to spend the next couple of months in their home. Begrudgingly, they agreed, but only because Sophie would be there, and they trusted her implicitly. I was ecstatic to spend the entire summer as a full-fledged adult, and I just knew it would be a special time. As fate would have it, that was the summer I met the man I was sure would end up being my prince, my soulmate. That summer, I met Marshall.

Chapter 6: Marshall

Although my mother had a difficult time accepting the fact that Quinton and I had broken up for good, I personally couldn't have been happier. I felt liberated in a way that I never thought I would feel without a boyfriend. Usually, after a breakup, I would feel like I was missing a limb or at least a digit. This time, I felt free. Moreover, Sophie and I were more than excited to stay in our apartment for the summer and slide into our senior year in style. We spent our days at the beach, working on our golden tans, and waiting tables at night to fund our weekend party-going.

Once of our favorite summertime hangouts was a bar downtown called Aqua. It was all underwater and mermaid themed. We made it a tradition to go there every Friday night. Fridays were called "ladies' night" and women got in for no cover charge. We would drink, flirt, and dance our hearts out into the wee hours of the morning. If we had any luck, we would find a cute boy to buy us drinks and leave with our phone numbers. It was at Aqua where I met the recently-graduated hunk of a man named Marshall. Marshall was something of a fish out of water at Aqua (pun intended). He didn't dance, he didn't drink, and he certainly didn't act a fool. He was there with some friends, but he was obviously not having a very good time.

I spotted him out of the corner of my eye, and something about him got my heart racing. Oh wait, it might have been his rugged good looks… or, I suppose it could have been the three vodka sodas I had guzzled. In any event, feeling no pain, my drunk ass decided to mosey on over and lay this brilliant line on him: "You gonna buy me a drink, or what?"

He looked at me, a little stunned, and said "what."

I thought he didn't hear me, so I repeated the question.

"Yeah," he said. "I heard you the first time. You asked me if I was going to buy you a drink or what. I am not going to buy you a drink, so I choose 'what.'"

Damn, this guy is weird.

Despite my initial confusion, I decided to press on. "Well, what now then?"

"Well, now we get out of here because it is loud and annoying in this hell hole, and I think we both need some fresh air. Would you like to walk outside with me and talk? Maybe we can grab a cup of coffee at the 24-hour diner across the street. I have heard they have great desserts."

I thought *What the hell*!? *Why not!* I found Sophie (who was grinding on the dancefloor with a guy she was sort of seeing off and on), and I told her I was going to drink some coffee at the diner with that person over there (pointing to Marshall who, at this point, looked like he wished he could call the cops and shut down this whole operation). Sophie admonished me to be careful but have fun, and we parted ways for the night.

Marshall gently but swiftly led me out of the club, and we walked over to the diner. I remember being preoccupied by the shoes he was wearing. "Are those cowboy boots?" I demanded.

"Uh, yeah," he replied, "Indeed they are."

"Are you a cowboy? I have never met a real cowboy. Do you live on a farm? Or, oh, wait. Is it a ranch? I mean, do you live on a ranch? Do you ride a horse?" I was full of questions.

Marshall chuckled and shook his head. "No, darlin. I just like cowboy boots."

Although I feigned extreme disappointment, I really didn't care one way or the other. This was how I flirted back then.

Marshall and I proceeded to spend the entire night at the diner. We talked about everything under the sun. We talked about the usual topics like where we grew up, what our families were like, where we worked, and what we did for fun. We also talked about deeper issues like what we thought happened to us when we die, what our dreams were for the future, and whether or not we believed in UFOs and aliens. (For the record, regarding the latter, the answer is yes. Absolutely. 100%.) It wasn't until the sun came up several hours later that we both realized we were completely exhausted. We had talked our throats raw, and our bellies were full of nothing but coffee and banana cream pie.

"May I drive you home?" he asked me.

Feeling extra emboldened due to our poignant and lengthy all-night conversation, I said "Sure! You may drive me to *your* home…"

So, there we went. We arrived at his tiny house on Saturday morning around 7 a.m. He lived alone, so we didn't worry about the noise we were making as we laughed and talked as we entered through the front door. As much as I would have loved to become intimate with him right then and there, I had to admit that we were both completely wiped out. Despite the fact that I could have fallen asleep standing up at this point, I knew I had to call Sophie really quickly, to let her know that I was fine but not coming home. I asked Marshall if I could use his phone to call my roommate, and he said "Of course!"

I dialed our apartment phone, and she answered it on the first ring. "Hello."

"Hey, Soph," I said, "it's me."

"Oh, thank God," she said, obviously concerned. "Are you okay? Are you safe? You have had me so stressed out! I started to fear that weird cop-looking guy took you to a deserted field and left you for dead."

"Oh, damn, Soph," I replied, apologetically, "I am so sorry. No," I chuckled, "there was thankfully none of that. Marshall and I just talked all night at that little diner, and then he brought me back to his house just now. We are going to take a nap and see where tomorrow, or actually today, leads us."

"Oooh, well, well, well. Sounds like you and Marshall really hit it off." I could hear the smile in her voice. "But wait!" she quickly continued, "How do I know you aren't calling me under duress? If he has kidnapped you, repeat the phrase 'Polly wants a cracker' and I will immediately call 9-1-1."

I giggled out loud and said, "Oh my gosh, Sophie. I sincerely appreciate your concern. I really do. But no, I am not going to repeat that phrase, and no, I have not been kidnapped."

I looked out of the corner of my eye, and I saw Marshall whip his head toward me, eyes wide, clearly concerned. I shook my head and mouthed "It's fine" and he seemed to relax a bit.

"Listen, Soph," I continued, "I had better go. I will see you soon. Have a great day, and I apologize, again, for making you worry."

"It's all right, Ann. Just please call me if you aren't planning to come home tonight. I really don't want another bout of restless sleep."

I promised to keep in touch, and I hung up the phone.

"So, she thought maybe I abducted you?" Marshall asked, cautiously but with a grin.

"Well," I replied, "I mean, she hoped that you didn't."

He laughed and told me that he was glad that I had such a thoughtful friend for a roommate. I agreed whole heartedly, and then I yawned and told him I was ready for bed if he was.

He concurred, and we awkwardly stripped down to our under garments. He asked if I wanted a t-shirt or something to sleep in, but it was rather warm, and I told him I was fine in my bra and underwear. "It's basically like sleeping in a swimsuit," I joked.

"Yeah, and I am in my swim trunks," he remarked, as he stood there in his boxer shorts.

Like a true gentleman, he asked if I wanted him to sleep on the couch. I told him that I would be happy for him to lay next to me in his bed, "Assuming that is," I remarked, "that you have no objections?"

He didn't object, so we laid down and we immediately fell fast asleep in his bed. We only slept for a couple of hours, however. We were both too wired from the excitement of our blossoming relationship, and we were too anxious to continue our getting-to-know-you phase to sleep any more. We got out of bed, and he made us some eggs and toast for brunch. We ended up spending the entire weekend at his place together. He let me wear his oversized sweats and t-shirt, and he even ran down to the corner pharmacy to buy me a toothbrush. That was the most exhilarating weekend I had ever spent in my entire life up to that point. I decided then and there that Marshall was the one. I didn't want to see anyone else ever again. Marshall was, as it turns out, my collegiate swan song.

***

Marshall was unlike anyone I had ever dated before. To be honest, he was unlike anyone I had ever known before. He was decidedly strait-laced, but not in a prudish or judgmental way. He grew up in a small town in rural Colorado, but he moved to Southern California in middle school. He recalled the time he spent in Colorado with great fondness.

"There is something devastatingly beautiful about the way the sun comes up over snowcapped mountains, Annabelle. It almost hurts to look at it. It makes you feel unworthy somehow… incredibly small and inconsequential. It is truly something to behold." His eyes almost watered as he recalled the sight.

I understood what he meant. I often felt that way when I looked out at the Pacific Ocean when it was calm, and the sun was just beginning to set. When I am in that place, I can almost feel my blood pressure lowering and my heart ready to burst with gratitude for this amazing planet we have the privilege to inhabit.

Marshall explained that his family moved to California due to his father's career. He was an officer in the United States Army. Marshall spoke reverently about the military and about his father.

Shortly after making the move from the mountains of Colorado to the desert of California, his father passed away, suddenly and unexpectedly, of a heart attack. Marshall was left to grow up very quickly. He was suddenly considered to be "the man of the house" at 13 years old. He took the job of looking after his mother and twin sister very seriously. Virginia, whom he called Ginny, was only 18 minutes his junior, but he cared for her as fervently as a mother hen cares for her chicks.

Despite the purported stress that military life put on his family, Marshall was proud of his father's service, and he admitted to feeling guilty that he opted not to enlist into the armed forces when he graduated from high school.

"My biggest regret," he would often say, "is not following in my father's footsteps."

Instead of pursuing military life, Marshall and Ginny went away to college together. Ginny studied biology, while Marshall studied architecture. They both graduated the year prior, and for the first time in their lives, they decided to live in separate cities. Ginny moved back home with their mother (who decided to return to Colorado Springs while the twins went away to college), but Marshall remained in California. He landed a job in an architectural firm just minutes from my university. Over the several months that we dated, I never observed him let more than two days go without speaking to either his mom or his sister on the phone. Despite the physical distance, they were a very tight-knit family.

I often marveled at how earnestly Marshall spoke about his parents. He loved them deeply, and he wasn't ashamed to let it be known. He truly taught me about living authentically. Although my parents drove me crazy from time to time, I believed they were good people who were doing the best that they could or knew how to do. Unlike me, Marshall didn't care what other people thought about him. He didn't fall prey to the expectations of the world or his peers. Certainly, his friends often tried to persuade him to drink alcohol or smoke weed or even light a cigarette, but he wouldn't do it. He didn't want to. He wasn't preachy about it; he just declined. Despite the occasional teasing, he held firm to his convictions, and he lived his truth. I have always admired him for that.

As one might expect, Mother was ecstatic. "Oh, Annabelle. I couldn't be happier for you. Sure, I thought you couldn't do better than Quinton, but boy was I wrong. Marshall is the real deal, honey. He is smart, accomplished, and he knows how to be a man. He is awfully handsome, too. I can almost see the darling faces of my beautiful grandchildren you two are destined to produce!"

"Ok, mom. Slow it down. You may be getting a little bit ahead of yourself. I am not sure we will be pumping out babies any time soon," I would chide. Though inside, I secretly hoped that she was right.

***

As my senior year started, I found it difficult to stay focused. All I wanted to do was go to school during the day, and then race over to Marsh's house as soon as he returned from work. I was still going to class, but keeping up with my homework was becoming a challenge. Regrettably, my grades were also starting to suffer.

"Listen up, Ann. You'd better snap out of it. I don't want to see you fuck around and fail all your classes. It's okay to spend time with Marshall; he's great. But damn it, Annabelle, get your shit together!" Sophie would scold.

"I know, I know," I would plead. "It's just a little case of senioritis. You'll see. I'll be fine. I will pass all of my classes with flying colors!" *Or, at least* walking *colors,* I would think to myself.

I continued, "Remember, Sophie: C's get degrees!" Lord, she hated it when I said that.

Luckily for me, Marshall was also as wise as Sophie. As soon as he noticed that I was spending more time at his place and less time at the library, he made a point of mentioning it. He did his best to keep me accountable to my studies. I had to hand it to him. Even though it affected him negatively, he wouldn't let me spend the night unless I showed him that I completed my schoolwork. And I couldn't just phone it in. He would read my papers and quiz me on content. Since I really enjoyed spending the night with him, I was motivated to keep my grades up. As the fall semester came to an end, I was proud to tell him that I finished my semester with three As and two Bs.

As we moved into Christmastime, I was feeling more and more sure that he was the one. "I really think this is it, Soph. I think I have finally found my prince," I declared.

Sophie agreed that he was pretty great, and she was happy that I found someone who not only made me extremely happy but also made me a better person.

"Hey, if he can get you to actually study, then what can I say? He is okay in my book. Plus, I have to admit that it has been pretty nice to be off duty this semester. Why do I always have to be the homework police, anyway?"

Sophie was right. She had spent the last three years nagging me to keep my head in the game. She would make sure my alarm was set, and then when I would hit snooze too many times, she would drag my ass out of bed and make sure I got to class. On the weekends, we weren't allowed to go out until we had put in at least an hour or two in the library. It is not hyperbole to say that Sophie is the only reason I graduated at all.

It's not that I didn't like school. I did. Once I was in class, I loved to learn about almost any subject. I found my professors to be super engaging, and the course content always left me intrigued and excited to learn more. It was just the waking up early and getting out of bed part that was annoying. I preferred to get up at the crack of noon. Oh, and the doing the homework and studying for tests parts really brought me down. I found that college was so much more difficult than high school. I suppose this should have been expected, but it kind of caught me off guard. I used to be able to make straight As in high school simply by attending class. Homework was an annoying time bandit, and it wasn't absolutely necessary to complete the homework in order to do well. I honestly never really knew what it meant to study. My thought process was: *What do you mean I need to spend time outside of class studying the material? The teacher just told me what I needed to know. Now I know it!*

As an end-of-the-semester and holiday present, Marshall invited me to accompany him to Colorado to visit his family for Christmas. I shrieked with delight as I told Sophie the big news.

"He asked me to meet his family!"

"That's amazing, Ann," Sophie quickly responded, "they are going to love you."

Although she said it in earnest, something about her comment gave me pause. I was so caught up in the idea that the act of inviting me to visit his family was proof that he took our relationship, and me, seriously. I hadn't taken it a step further to realize that this would be his family's first opportunity to meet and (let's face it) evaluate me.

"Oh, shit!" I blurted out. "What if they don't like me, Soph?" I suddenly felt panicked.

"Oh, stop it. What's not to like? You are amazing, Annie. Oh, of course they will like you!"

I realized that this was the first time I would be meeting a boyfriend's family. I mean, obviously I knew Oz' family. We were children when we started dating. But this time… this was serious. I knew I had to make a good impression. I couldn't let their first impression of me be their *last* impression.

Despite my better judgment, I called my mother for advice. I was mildly concerned that she would be upset that I would not be home for the holidays. This would be the first time in my entire life that my parents wouldn't have their only kid home with them to celebrate. Boy, was I wrong.

"Oh, my goodness. This is fantastic! I am so excited for you, Annabelle. This is a very important moment. This could be make or break." My mother was all aflutter, pleased to no end that Marshall had invited me home.

In a fury of excitement, she began listing off all of the crucial elements of a successful family visit.

"You must bring a couple of nice outfits. Don't show up in your ripped up jeans and flannel shirt, Annabelle. I know you think it looks *cool,* but you are not going out with your college friends. You are meeting his mother." I could sense the worry in her voice as she spoke.

"Do you have any dresses with lace or a nice ruffle? Never mind, you can borrow something of mine."

"Oh my God, Mother," I snapped. "We are not going to a tea party at Buckingham Palace. They are normal people. They probably wear flannel shirts themselves."

Despite my confident tone, I was wondering if they did, in fact, wear flannel.

Mom went on and on about how to dress, how to act, what to say, what not to say, and when and how to eat. "Whatever you do, do NOT take a bite before Marshall and his mother take a bite. Do you understand? You don't want to look like a ravenous pig, dear."

"Mom! What do you think I am going to do? Throw my plate on the floor, turn it into a trough, and smash my face into the mashed potatoes? Give me some credit, will you? I think I know how to behave like a human." I was beginning to get offended by this line of questioning and admonishment.

Annoyed, my mother replied, slowly, and in a tone that suggested she was annoyed that I was not taking her advice seriously. "Yes, dear. I know you won't fall onto your hands and knees to devour your dinner. All I am saying is that you need to remain courteous and respectful. This is his mother's home, and Marshall is the man of the house. They deserve the respect of taking the first bite. It would be wise of you to remember that." She seemed to wonder how I didn't know all of this already.

grandmother"Oh!" she seemed to suddenly remember something very important, and she continued, "and whatever you do, be sure to thank Marshall *publicly* for the opportunity to visit. You want to communicate to his mother that you are deferential and that you know how to treat a man. This will be her primary concern for her one and only son's love interest."

"Got it," I replied. "I will make sure to fall to my hands and knees, kiss his feet, and thank him for this precious opportunity." I was laying the sarcasm on thick.

Clearly exasperated by my over-exaggerated mockery, my mother just took a deep breath and calmly replied, "Annabelle, stop. I do not want to get into it with you like this. Just please realize that I love you, and I want this visit to go well for you. That's it. That's all I am trying to do."

Damn, I thought. She knew how to hit me where it hurt.

Feeling rather regretful for my bratty and combative rhetoric, I replied, "I'm sorry, Mom. I know. I'm just nervous. I don't mean to be a jerk. I really don't."

She replied, as if she seemingly forgot all about our squabble, "Never mind all that, Annabelle. Let's talk about what you can bring his mother for a hostess gift."

We spent the next few minutes debating the pros and cons of the most appropriate item to bring. "What's better?" she wondered aloud, "A nice bottle of wine or a tasteful houseplant?" We settled on a bottle of wine, as I couldn't easily travel with either of these items, and I would most likely need to pick something up at the airport when we landed. I figured a bottle of vino would be easier to procure than a plant at Denver International.

"Ok, good idea," she replied. "Be sure to find something moderately priced. You don't want to be extra cheap. That communicates that she is not valuable to you. However, you don't want to buy anything too exorbitant, as that has the potential to look too showy and gratuitous."

Mom always thought of everything.

"Perfect, Mom," I replied. "Since I am basically broke, moderate works well for me."

We chit-chatted for a few more minutes, and then she told me she needed to go to begin preparing dinner. "You know how Dad gets if he doesn't eat by 5:00 p.m.," she chided.

She admonished me a couple more times to watch my manners and look presentable while away with Marshall. I agreed to be on my very best behavior, and then I hung up the phone, a little sorry I had called her in the first place. If I thought I was a tad bit nervous before we spoke, I was now in a full-blown panic. *What if they don't like me? What if I am a disappointment? What if they don't drink wine?* These questions and many more circled throughout my mind for hours. For the most part, there was only one main question that turned my stomach into knots: *Would Marshall ever stay with a woman his mother and sister didn't approve of?* I was clearly working myself up into a frenzy.

Luckily, like always, Sophie was there to calm me down. "Relax, Ann" she soothed, "I am 100% certain they will adore you. Besides, they seem like genuinely nice people, and Marshall is obviously crazy about you. You have nothing to worry about, Annabelle. I promise."

As much as I wanted to believe her, doubt always found a way to creep in. But fortunately, it turned out that despite all of my anxiety, packing and repacking dozens of outfits, fretting about what to say and what not to say, the visit went extremely well. His mother and sister were lovely, and they treated me with kindness and with the same genuine, trademark care that Marshall always demonstrated. I finally knew where he got it. Oh! And yes, they even wore flannel. *Take that, Mom,* I remember thinking to myself with a chuckle.

This trip to his home is also where he first told me that he loved me. We were sitting on the living room floor, leaning up against the couch, looking at their beautiful family Christmas tree. There were dozens of colorful lights and ornaments that told the story of Marshall's life. Some were very old, antique ornaments that used to don his grandparents' tree, he told me. Others were handmade treasures that he and Ginny made back in grade school. As we gazed into the lights, almost becoming mesmerized by the beauty of it all, I leaned my head on his shoulder, and he wrapped me under his arm. He smoothed the hair away from my face and nestled his mouth into my ear. "I love you, Annabelle," he whispered. Without skipping a beat, I replied in kind. "I love you too."

We came back from Colorado, exhilarated, and falling more deeply for one another. As I prepared for the start of the spring semester, my final semester in college, I fantasized about a life with him. I wondered if he would propose to me after graduation. Would it be a long engagement? Would we elope? No, we definitely wouldn't elope. Mother would be furious if she couldn't witness her baby girl stepping into her destiny and becoming a wife. Still, the thoughts of life with Marshall brought me endless joy and rapt anticipation. Unbeknownst to me, this elation would soon turn to despair.

***

I remember it like it was yesterday. I had just woken up on that otherwise mundane January morning, but this day was different than others. People all around my apartment complex were running around the courtyard yelling about war in the Middle East. I heard phrases like "Shock and Awe" and "Fuck Saddam Hussein" being slung around, and I was nervous but anxious to find out what the hell was going on.

"Turn on the TV, Soph!" I yelled from the front porch. "I think something big is going on in the Gulf."

As we learned from the news, Operation Desert Storm had been launched under the leadership of our then U.S. President, George H. W. Bush. It was a surreal moment, watching a live feed of the conflict on TV. I remember seeing Middle Eastern skies obscured by the thick, black smoke of war. Massive tanks were cutting through the deserts, surrounded by sand and blasts of fire. It was a particularly confusing and worrisome sight. This was the first time that my generation had seen this level of conflict. Sure, we heard stories of our grandparents' generation who fought valiantly in World War II. Many of us had parents who also survived war in Korea or Vietnam. But for my generation, Generation X as they came to call us, this was the first time we saw war first-hand. It was brought directly into our homes courtesy of CNN. The livestreamed horrors of war were pumped out through the airwaves 24/7. It was honestly an uneasy and sobering time to be alive.

Unsurprisingly, word of war spread quickly, and withing minutes, Marshall was calling. His voice was shaking as he described the conflict to me, sharing the history and nuances that I hadn't yet been exposed to. I could feel the pain in his voice, but I also heard something else. It was a sentiment I did not want to hear. I heard yearning.

Predictably, Marshall spent the weekend obsessing about the conflict. He was glued to the television and only left the living room to use the restroom and to call his family. He spoke in hushed tones, and I became increasingly uneasy with the situation. I knew in my heart that something important was about to happen. The following week, I got my answer. Marshall decided to follow in his father's footsteps after all. He enlisted in the Army.

I felt like the wind had been knocked out of me when he told me. It was cognitive dissonance for sure. How could he enlist in the service just when we were falling in love?

Despite my cries and my pleas for him to reconsider, Marshall was resolute.

"I have to do this, Annie. I just have to."

"No, Marshall. You DON'T have to. You absolutely do not have to do this." I couldn't believe what was happening.

I continued, "I thought you loved me. I thought you wouldn't want to leave me."

He quieted his voice and looked me square in the eyes. "Both of those things are true, Annabelle. I do love you, and I don't want to leave you." I could tell this was a difficult conversation for both of us.

Though shaken, I continued to plead: "Then don't go. Stay here with me. You have too much to lose. You can't just walk away from everything, Marsh. You can't just walk away from your friends, from your career.... from me...."

Marshall grew quiet, and he thought earnestly before he spoke. "Annabelle, I know I can't make you understand, but this is not only something that I have to do; it is also something that I need to do." After a long exhale, he added, "It is something that I *am going* to do."

If I knew anything about Marshall, it is that he meant what he said and he did what he wanted. He was never going to be talked out of doing anything he had set his mind to doing. Nonetheless, I threw up a hail Mary as a last-ditch effort to salvage this crisis. "Well, Marshall, I guess you have a choice to make. You either choose me, or you choose the Army."

I regretted it as soon as it escaped my lips, but it was too late to take it back. It was out there, hanging thick between us like the black smoke I saw on my television set.

He pulled no punches when he responded to what must have felt to him like the ultimatum of a recalcitrant child. "I am choosing duty, Annabelle. I am choosing what's right. I am not trying to hurt you, but I cannot sit back and watch this conflict from the comfort of my living room. I need to be there and live out what I have always known is my destiny. This is bigger than you and me, Annie. I hope you can forgive me one day, but I am going. I will always remember you fondly."

And with that, he was gone. Gone, too, were my hopes that I would become Mrs. Marshall Brooks, wife of a handsome, honorable, and talented architect. Instead, I would remain who I always was... who it felt I would always be: Annabelle, the unloved, and the unchosen.

Chapter 7: Homecoming

My final semester of college became unbearable. I fell into a deep depression, and it took all my energy to get up, put on something other than my filthy, ice cream-stained sweatpants, and attend my classes. I walked around the apartment like a zombie, and I rarely went out for fun. All I wanted to do was lay in my bed, with the covers up and over my head, trying to will myself to sleep. Slumber was the only activity that offered me an escape from my melancholy, but sleep was, unfortunately, elusive. Daily living felt like an impossible chore. I missed Marshall, but I also loathed him. How could he have left me? How come I wasn't enough? Even Sophie had trouble keeping me on track.

"You can't keep doing this, Ann" Sophie would say with a tone that suggested she was equally worried about and annoyed with me.

"I don't see the point of school anymore, Soph" I would reply in earnest. "Marshall is gone. The world is on fire. Everything is shit."

Sophie would sit at the edge of my bed, gently place her hand on my shoulder and say with as much love and understanding as she was able to muster, "That may be true, Annie. But guess what? Here is another way to look at it: You are here. The world is your oyster. Everything is possible." And, for good measure, she would often throw in a "Now get your sorry ass out of bed and go to class, or you will live to regret it," as she tickled me in my ribs—my mortal weakness.

I should have been embarrassed that Sophie was reduced to taking care of me like I was one of her baby sisters. I also should have been able to navigate this loss in a more mature and productive way. It was just another breakup, after all. Right? No, apparently not. For some reason, this one hit me exceptionally hard. But looking back, I realize it was more than just the breakup. I suspect it also had to do with the fact that I saw the end of college looming just in front of me. While some may argue that graduating from college is solely a moment to celebrate, that is often not the whole story. Yes, it is an accomplishment that denotes a significate achievement; it marks the successful end of exams, term papers, and pop quizzes. These are certainly all valid and sensible reasons to celebrate. However, for many young people, I believe that graduating from college is also an extremely difficult and confusing time. It certainly was for me. I suddenly found myself at the precipice of true adulthood, and I no longer had a path to follow. I was expected to just reach this cliff and jump, but, like many other young graduates, I did not have a parachute. Marshall was supposed to be my parachute. He was supposed to be my next step in a predetermined path. Let's face it: up until this point in my life, I always had a prescriptive map to follow. Done with elementary school? Congratulations! Enter Junior High. Graduated from high school? Super! Welcome to college. Finishing college? Oh shit. Now what?

Luckily, Sophie never made me feel like a helpless, bratty child. Although she had her own tests to study for and her own essays to write, she found the time and the energy to hold me accountable and keep me afloat. She took me under her wing and made sure I did what I needed to do. She ensured that I attended my classes, and she even drove me to and from work. And she did it all without shame or condemnation. She absolutely rescued me from the funk I was in, and she saved me from inevitable ruin. Again, that is not hyperbole. By the grace of Sophie, I ended up finishing my final semester. It wasn't necessarily pretty, but I finished. That May, she and I graduated from our university. I certainly didn't break any academic records, nor was I handed any special awards, but I passed my classes, and I finished in four years. Given the hurdle I endured in my final semester, this was no small feat. Sophie graduated at the top of our class, of course, and I couldn't have been more proud of her. She was, and continues to be, a genuine superstar.

***

Despite our different rankings, we both felt incredibly accomplished, and we came to terms with the fact that college life was ending. In time, I started to look forward to creating my life after college. The pain of Marshall slowly began to fade, and by the time we packed up our things and said goodbye to our off-campus apartment for the last time, hope was starting to glimmer within me. Unable to stay in the big, cosmopolitan city of our university, we headed back to our hometown in the suburbs and found a little apartment to rent. The place was tiny, but it was brand new, and we loved the surrounding neighborhood. It happened to be a bit out of our price range, but we cashed in all of our graduation gifts for the first and last month's rent and security deposit, and we rolled the dice. Despite the lack of job prospects and little to no money in our savings, we somehow felt excited and hopeful about our future. Heck, as long as I had Sophie in my corner, I felt like I could do anything and be anything.

Unlike many of our friends who graduated college with their "forever loves," Sophie and I were decidedly single. We tried to not let this upset us too much though. Despite the occasional sorrow we felt in graduating without significant others in our lives, we attempted to find strength in our independence and tried to convince ourselves that we didn't need a man to make us happy. We used to turn our noses up when we would receive yet another wedding invitation in the mail, and we would play Lynyrd Skynyrd on our little table-top stereo and sing the lyrics to "Free Bird" at the top of our lungs:

Cause I'm as free as a bird now
And this bird you cannot change

We tried to convince ourselves that the world was genuinely full of possibility, and we tried to manifest the truth that we were marching towards the land of inevitable success and ultimate happiness. According to my parents, however, we were on the fast-track to spinster-ville.

"Well, I hope you are happy, Annabelle," my mother would chime as she hung her head in defeat. "You had four good years to find your husband, and you wasted them. How could you have been so careless, sweetie? Why did you and darling Nash break up? And what about that Quinton? Is he still single? I will never understand why you let that one get away. And Marshall! My word, Annabelle. What a man. What a patriot. What a hero! Why didn't you tell him you would wait for him, dear?"

"Mother, drop it!" I would snap. I made vain attempts at explaining to her that those men weren't right for me and that, furthermore, I didn't need a man to be complete. I tried to convince her that I was working on myself and finding my own place in the world.

"I will tell you where your place is, young lady; your place is in the home, where your mother, grandmother, and great-grandmother have done their very best work. I don't see why you feel you need to go all *Mary Tyler Moore* out there."

I almost laughed out loud at this preposterous notion. Did my mother, grandmother and great-grandmother work their asses off in the home? A resounding *HELL YES!* they did. Was it their "best" work? I guess you'd have to define "best."

I have distinct memories of summertime family get-togethers at my great-grandmother's house. She was in her mid to late 80's, living in the San Gabriel Valley of Los Angeles. In the summertime, temperatures could climb well into triple digits. She would be slaving away in the kitchen—the oven and stove on full tilt heating her tiny 1,000 square foot house up to intolerable temperatures–while my grandmother, her sisters, and my mother were scurrying around, filling up their husbands' and sons' and grandsons' glasses of iced tea and lemonade, and preparing the backyard picnic tables for the feast that was to come. This meant endless trips back and forth from the kitchen to the backyard, up and down three or four steps from the landing, through an unevenly paved side yard, out to the picnic tables, holding hot and heavy casserole dishes and bowls, to make sure that everything was brought from the house to the yard at just the right temperature. Even my female cousins and I were expected to participate.

"Annie, you grab the napkins and the silverware; Alison, you get the placemats and the extra cups," Grandma would admonish us, as she clearly became suspicious that we were about to peel off and play whiffle ball with the boys.

Alison and I would give each other side eye and hang our heads in disappointment. "Okay, Grandma," we would moan as we complied with her request. Indeed, we were hoping to peel off to play whiffle ball with the boys.

Where was everyone else while this 'best work' was taking place? Ah, the men were relaxing under the big oak tree in the backyard, playing cards or shooting the breeze; the boys were playing whiffle ball, or hide and seek, or marbles, or taking turns swinging on the big, black tire swing. The menfolk were living in the lap of luxury, one might argue, while the womenfolk worked their fingers to the bone to make sure the kings had their spoils.

The best part (and by "best" I mean the absolute worst) is that when all the preparations were complete, the food was served, and everyone was ready to dig into this glorious feast, the men were given the best seats at the picnic table and were served their meals first. Naturally, the women did the honors. Even the boys were given folding chairs at the ends of the table, and they ate with their older kin. Where were the women and girls placed? We were sitting on any makeshift seat we could find (a tree stump, the edge of the retaining wall, or a car bumper were the most coveted spots), plates on our laps, woofing down our food quickly so we could at least eat *some* of it before the men needed one of us to run into the house to fetch them seconds.

To my recollection, nobody ever complained. It frankly didn't seem odd or unusual. It didn't even seem unjust. It was, simply, the way it was.

I shook my head in disbelief at that memory. *What the hell?* I thought to myself. *Is that the* best *work I am going to do?*

"Listen Annabelle," Mother startled me from my daydream, "why don't you just move back in with your father and me, and we will help you find your one true love. As much as we adore Sophie—and you *know* that we do—I think it would be wise to stay close to home and save some money. More importantly, I don't want to see you become distracted. You really do need to focus on finding Mr. Right, my dear."

Oh. My. God. The thought of moving back home was unbearable and impossible in the same way that crawling back into her uterus would be. No, I was not going to go backwards. And the thought of my mother helping me to find my "one true love?" Oh, Jesus. Kill me now. How would that even work? I can picture it perfectly: *Margaret, have you seen my lovely Annabelle lately? She is just darling. How is your dear Kevin? Is he seeing anyone special these days? I have a feeling about those two…* Oh, hell no, Mom. Kevin? KEVIN? The kid who ate his boogers in 4th grade? Oh, God. Seriously, though. Vile! Absolutely not. Hard no.

"Look, Mom," I tried to say as lovingly as possible, "I sincerely appreciate your concern. I really do. However, this is something that I need to do for myself. I need to stand on my own two feet. I need to understand who I am and where I fit in this world. As I learned in my Psychology 100 class (side note: I found it usually helped to quote some 'authority' on a subject, though my typical go-to was Sally Jessy Raphael, my mom's favorite), you have to love yourself before anyone else can love you. I am in the process of learning to love myself, Mom."

"Ugh," she said with disgust. "I knew sending you to a liberal college was a mistake. I told your father you needed to go to a nice, private, Christian school with good family values. But he insisted that since you 'earned' a spot in that so-called 'top university,' that you shouldn't let that opportunity pass you by. Well, if you ask me, you may have let your opportunity to find your one true love pass you by. Honestly, I think he just wanted bragging rights at the water cooler and easy access to the football games," she said as she continued to straighten the tablecloth she was replacing from the laundry. "Besides," she continued, "You are so pretty, Annabelle. Why did you need to go to college anyway!?" She seemed sincerely perplexed.

I fought my urge to condemn the premise of her last question, but I realized it would be pointless. She certainly wasn't asking me in earnest. At this point, I just wanted to calm her down and end the conversation.

"Oh, mom. I will find my Mr. Right when the *time* is right. You'll see," I tried to feign confidence.

"I certainly hope so, dear. You only have so many good child-bearing years, and the clock is ticking. Many of your friends [one could substitute the word "competitors" here] opted to not waste, eh, er, I mean *spend*, four years away at college, so they have snapped up many of the most desirable men in this area. I just want you to be happy, Annabelle..." her voice trailed off as she looked, somewhat despondently, into the void that was in front of her and, apparently, all around me.

"I know, Mom. I get it. But please don't worry. I am happy. I will be happy. I promise" I said calmly, trying to reassure her.

She snapped back into focus and quipped "Tick tock, Annabelle" and went back to setting the table for dinner.

The sad reality is that, although I worked overtime to reassure my mother that I was in a good place, I was mostly trying to convince myself. I desperately wanted to be the free, independent, headstrong, self-assured, single woman who was kicking ass and taking names that I tried to envision myself to be. The unfortunate truth was, however, that I wasn't so sure. When I looked in the mirror, I saw a lone woman. I couldn't seem to kick the notion that I was less than if I was single. Was Mother right? Did I waste my time in college? Should I have told Marshall I would wait for him? Should I have given Quinton more grace? As much as I wanted to deny it, I was definitely a victim of the programming of my youth. I was utterly convinced that I needed my prince. So, I redoubled my efforts and set my sights on finding him. As it turns out, Sophie found him for me.

Chapter 8: Jefferson

All things considered, life was going fairly well for Sophie and me. I found a job at a local restaurant called *Sunshine Grill.* It was a family establishment, all California-themed. It was a pretty large space with three different and distinct rooms, each decorated in a motif that represented the various environments of California. There was a desert-inspired room that featured cacti and light, neutral colors like browns, beiges, and sage greens. There was also a beach-themed room with wicker and bamboo finishings and more vibrant colors like various shades of blues and yellows. My favorite was the mountain-themed room with rich mahogany furniture and warm colors like deep greens and off whites. Within a couple of weeks of working there, I quickly moved from hostess to waitress, thanks to my *Seaside* experience. While it was a bit discouraging that I was still waiting tables despite my college degree, I couldn't really complain. Waiting tables had good hours (meaning, I didn't have to get up early), and I always came home with a wad of cash in my pocket thanks to my tips. Sure, I was half-heartedly sending out resumes for more "professional" jobs in my field--copywriting, editing, freelance writing, and even tutoring—but, somehow, my heart wasn't in it. Despite my insistence that I was happy waiting tables and that it was only a matter of time before I landed a more significant job, my mother never seemed satisfied. She continued to frequently express her displeasure with my choice to attend college at all, suggesting that it was a sincere waste of time. She would also regularly ask me: "What can you do with an English major anyway, Annabelle?"

"Well, Mom, apparently you can wait tables" I would retort, sarcastically.

"Hmph. Makes no difference. You are just staying busy until you meet the love of your life, and he rescues you from the drudgery of restaurant life and places you in your castle."

Though part of me truly appreciated her unwavering commitment to the belief that I was destined to find my prince, she couldn't hide the fear and uncertainty in her voice if she tried.

"Yeah, so I can be a cook AND a waitress…and do it all for free." I couldn't help myself.

Completely disregarding the sardonic truth of what I had just said, she would retort: "Honestly, Annabelle. You need to watch that sassy tone of yours. No man is going to want to hear it."

In her defense, she was probably right. From what I could tell, the men I knew did seem to prefer women who spoke less and smiled more.

I remember my first day on the job as the hostess at *Sunshine Grill*. "Ok, Annie," my manager, Mike, told me.

"Just be sure to smile at the customers and make them feel welcome."

Sure! I thought. *How hard can that be? Stand around and smile. Easy. I've got this.* Yet, whenever I was caught looking you know, normal, Mike would come along, sidle up to me and remind me that I was much more attractive when I smiled.

"Come on, now, Annie. Where's that smile?" he would cajole.

"Sorry, Mike," I would respond without missing a beat. "I forgot that I was happy."

"Oh, Annie, you are too much," he would say with a chuckle.

No, Mike, I would think to myself. *Apparently, I am not.*

So, yeah. This is how I spent the better part of a year post-college: waiting tables, watching my sassy tone, remembering to smile, and simultaneously both enjoying my autonomy and secretly praying for a man. It was a confusing time for me.

While I was busy waiting tables at *Sunshine Grill,* Sophie landed an office job at a lawyer's office. She was considering law school, and her father had a friend who owned his own firm. He arranged for Sophie to start a paid internship at their offices so she could see if this career was indeed a good fit. Sophie began working typical Monday through Friday 8 am -5 pm hours, while I mostly worked nights and weekends. For the first time in the nearly 10 years I had known her, our schedules did not match up.

Not having Sophie there for me throughout the day added to my stress and my melancholy. Sophie was the only person, it seemed, who didn't find me a terrible disappointment. Although I was happy for her and proud of these steps she was taking to pursue her dream, I couldn't help but feel sorry for myself that my best friend seemed to be moving on without me. Luckily, we remained roommates, and we cherished those precious times every now and again when we had time to just hang out together, laugh, and reconnect.

Furthermore, I marveled at how Sophie's parents seemed to remain beautifully oblivious to her *single* lifestyle. They appeared to embrace her desire to have a career, and they never put pressure on her to find a soulmate. I couldn't help but feel envious that Sophie was able to simply live her life, outside of the microscope of her parents' prying (and, what's worse) judgmental eyes. I regularly asked how she managed to stay off their radar in this way.

"Annie," she would argue, "I have four younger siblings. My parents are in over their heads with those rug rats. They also have the restaurant to occupy their time. They can't be bothered to micromanage my love life or my lifestyle."

Whether it was intentional, or just a happy little accident (as good ol' Bob Ross used to say), that kind of anonymity seemed like a dream to me. I often envisioned her anonymity to be like a big, fluffy blanket, keeping her both warm and safe as well as hidden from her parents' interfering eyes. Oh, how I wished I had such a blanket, such privacy.

***

Throughout that year, I continued to work at *Sunshine Grill*. As I earned more seniority there, I was able to gain a bit more control over my schedule. I took on a few more weekday shifts and was able to take some Saturdays off. One of these occasions, Sophie came home on a Friday, mid-afternoon from the law firm and excitedly proclaimed, "Cancel your plans for tomorrow night. We have dates!"

"Perfect! I don't have any plans. Who are the lucky bastards, anyway?" I inquired with delight. I hadn't been on a proper date in months, and I was beginning to feel like a pariah.

"Ok, so there's this guy who just landed a junior associate position. His name is Jefferson, but he goes by 'Jefe.' I guess he was the president of his fraternity at some Ivy League university and the name sort of stuck. He was having lunch with his college roommate, and I happened to run into them. The friend was really cute, and we totally hit it off. He asked if he could see me tomorrow night, and I said only if I can bring my bestie, Annabelle. Honestly, I was a little scared to go out with this guy without you, Ann. He is, like, *so* cute. Anyway, he said Jefferson would go too and we could double date. You HAVE to go, Annie. You HAVE to."

I feigned exasperation, but I was definitely excited to go. "Of course," I said. "Anything for my bestie."

***

Saturday arrived and Sophie and I immediately shifted into go mode. We ran to our closets and started pulling out clothing options. We each tried on probably five or six different outfits, all the while running back and forth between each other's rooms, asking for advice: "Which shoes should I wear with this dress?" "Does this shirt go with these pants?" "Does this skirt make my ass look too big?" We finally settled on our attire, and we spent the next hour or so finishing up our hair and our makeup. By the time the guys came to pick us up to take us to the new, trendy bar in town, we were looking good and feeling good.

That night turned out to be like none I had ever experienced before. Jefferson was simply exquisite. He was about 5 years my senior, and he was extremely good looking. He honestly looked as though he had just stepped out of a *GQ* magazine. He clearly was no stranger to the gym, and he wore his designer button-down shirt tight over his well sculpted chest. He had playful green eyes that seemed to twinkle as he spoke. He wore his dirty blond hair in a shaggy but manicured cut that seemed to scream *I am young, hot, and playful.... but I am also gainfully employed.*

Jefferson and his friend, Raymond (whom everyone called Ray Ray), had apparently been friends since childhood. Ray Ray was the quintessential surfer boy. He had grown up with Jefferson in a coastal town in Southern California, and he was known up and down the state for his surfing prowess. Signed at a young age by a major surfing label, Ray Ray was ostensibly quite the catch. "A sun-kissed hottie" as *Surfing* magazine reportedly referred to him, Ray Ray was an easy-going, laid-back dude who liked to walk around barefoot, play frisbee on the sand when not surfing, and make his own fruit smoothies. Quite his opposite, Jefferson preferred to shop at expensive, designer stores, drive his BMW along the coast, and check up on his investments in his free time. Despite their differences, Jeffy (as I called him) and Ray Ray were very good friends.

Once at the bar, Jefferson and I paired off at a two-person table, and Sophie and Ray Ray paired off at another. I was anxious to get to know this man a little bit better. From the looks of it, Sophie was just as eager to get to know Ray Ray.

"So, Annie, tell me about yourself," Jefe began. I was a little taken-aback at that seemingly innocuous question. *Tell you about myself?* I repeated in my mind. What was there to tell? I was a 23-year-old woman, recently graduated, waiting tables at a local mom and pop restaurant, trying to find my footing in a cold and broken world, while also looking for my prince to carry me away from it all. Somehow, that seemed like an overly complicated and awkward response to his breaking-the-ice question, so I opted for a cool: "Um, well, you know… I recently graduated and am now just living the dream."

Jefferson offered a casual but authentic chuckle and replied, "Ah, yes. Living that California dream. I hear ya. I am doing the same thing. What was your major in school?"

Oh, my. Another question about me. This was extremely unexpected. He was really hitting it out of the park. Usually, guys who look like him with a job like his only have one thing on their mind: themselves. Two questions about little ol' me? This was unprecedented.

"Oh, well, I was an English major. So, yeah. Now I am waiting tables."

To that, Jefferson leaned his head back and gave a deep belly laugh. "I love it. You're playing into the stereotype in a clever and self-deprecating way. You're funny, Annabelle."

It was curious how he tended to narrate my responses in a way that was both playful but also painfully accurate. Something about his attentiveness and the way he proclaimed what I am made me a little light-headed, even if he did call me Annabelle.

"It's just Annie, actually."

"Oh. Okay, sorry. Annie, then. For the record, Annabelle is a beautiful name. But I like Annie as well. Makes me feel like Daddy Warbucks." He winked, to really bring it home.

Now, for the record, this should have been my first red flag. Nobody should refer to himself as Daddy Warbucks in casual conversation on a first date and get away with it.

However, it was just quirky enough to make me giggle and mischievous enough to disarm me in a way that made me feel something entirely unexpected. I suddenly felt *seen.* I hadn't thought about the name Annabelle being beautiful, let alone *mine.* I had always felt like I was borrowing the name from the real Annabelle… the regal Annabelle… the *presidential* Annabelle.

"It's a hard knock life after all," I added.

"Oh, Annie!" he said as he laughed with full gusto. "You're too much."

***

To say that the next year of my life wasn't completely surreal would be a lie. I was suddenly introduced to a whole new level of wealth and sophistication. Growing up in a modest 3-bedroom, 2-bathroom house in a working-class neighborhood, the wealthiest person I knew growing up was the guy down the street whose stepdad owned a car dealership and had commercials on the local cable station. They were so well-to-do that they put a second-story addition onto their house, and they built a swimming pool in their backyard. They were suburban celebrity for sure.

But Jefferson…. Jefferson was next level. He had a condo that actually faced the Pacific Ocean. He owned furniture that he bought directly from a fancy, designer store. (Honestly, I didn't realize you could even do that. Every single piece of furniture I had ever owned from childhood through young adulthood had either been purchased from a garage sale or thrift store or was handed down from my grandparents.) He ate at restaurants that served lobster and champagne, and he never even used a coupon at the grocery store. I remember one time he accompanied me to the local supermarket, and as I was about to pay, I proudly whipped out a $1 off coupon. He was shocked, and, in retrospect, maybe a little embarrassed, and asked me what I was doing. "Saving a buck on these groceries, buddy" I replied, with satisfaction.

"Oh, Annie," he said with a half-hearted grin, "you're too much."

Little did I know back then that being "too much" was definitely code for "not enough."

Despite our obvious differences (he, an Ivy League lawyer who grew up with a silver spoon in his mouth, and me, a waitress with a college degree and a penchant for bargain hunting), we seemed to work. We had fun when we were together, and we fortunately had good conversation AND good sex.

I loved the fact that he exuded confidence. He seemed to be the perfect blend between Nash and Quinton. He had the charisma of Nash, but none of the sexual predator-ness. Similarly, he had the civility of Quinton, but none of the oh-my-God-I-am-a-gentle-weeping-flower-ness.

Did I see any red flags? I mean, well, maybe. For one: I didn't know any of his friends except for Ray Ray. According to Jeffy, none of his friends were really worth knowing. "They are more like colleagues than friends, Annie," he would say when I pleaded to meet his people.

"But you spend so much time with them, Jeff," I said. "I want to know who is taking away my guy for hours on end every day and some weekends!"

"Babe," he would say, slowly and lovingly, "they are not important. You are the only important person in my life."

Damn, he knew how to melt my heart.

Even Ray Ray, Jeffy said, was basically expendable. Sure, they had been friends since childhood, but really, they had little in common anymore. They only got together once in a blue moon when Ray Ray would come back into town for a surfing competition. Otherwise, Raymond was never in one place for very long. He surfed the entire world, following the wind where it took him.

Poor Sophie found that out the hard way. She had really taken a shine to him. After that first date, they were inseparable for the entire week. She called out sick to work and they hung out at the beach all day, every day. He was even teaching her to surf. She was truly smitten. Unfortunately, and (as we realized in retrospect) unsurprisingly, after that week, he told her that he needed to head over to New South Whales for the Australian Surfing Championships. She was crestfallen.

"What the fuck? How can he just up and leave? We have bonded!" she pleaded to Jeffy and me.

"That's Ray Ray," Jefferson replied. "It's who he is; it's what he does."

"Well, it's fucked," Sophie said. I could tell she was sincerely hurt. "Fuck him then," she continued. "I hope he surfs himself into a kangaroo pouch and hops away to the moon!"

"I'm not sure that's how surfing works, Soph," I joked, "but I hope he does too."

As I sat with Jefferson that night, I reiterated how sorry I was for Sophie. "On one hand, I am sorry she ever met him. She doesn't deserve this kind of heartbreak."

"On the other hand," he continued, "it's a damn good thing they did meet. Otherwise, I wouldn't have met you."

As much as my heart broke for Sophie, I couldn't help but feel elated for myself. Little did I know that elation, like most things, doesn't last.

***

As we neared our one-year anniversary, nobody was happier than my mom.

"Well, sweetheart," she said proudly, "you did it! You reeled in the big one!"

Side note: I always found it odd that my mother, the woman who loved animals more than people, would regularly use cliches that suggested their painful demise. Just another reminder that we are all subject to our programming. We breathe it in like the air all around us. It is insidious, really. We become who we are programmed to become. This programming comes in the form of our cultures, our entertainment, our education... we see it in every television ad, in every magazine article, in every casual and corporate conversation. We are swimming in it and drinking it in all at once. I, too, was subject to this programming. My program plan was simple: find your Prince Charming, and all will be right in the universe.

"Yeah," I responded. "He is really great. I mean, he definitely is very busy with work, so I don't get to see him as much as I would like, but I guess that just goes with the territory."

"Well, yes, darling. He is a very busy man with a very important job. Corporate lawyers don't always have the luxury of spare time, but you know he makes up for it in other ways." She meant his very generous gifts.

I can't say that I didn't like his gifts. I did. Although, part of me felt weird accepting such lavish and expensive tokens of his affection. Who am I? I felt like an imposter. How am I, little middle-class Annie, sporting designer clothes and expensive jewelry, anyway? The other part of me felt exhilarated to be holding my very first Prada handbag. Honestly, I didn't even know that expensive purses were called "bags." Jeffy taught me that. He once asked me if I had a favorite bag designer. I didn't know what to say, so I just blurted out "Hefty." Once again, he laughed his infectious belly laugh and retorted, "Annie, you're too much!"

"What is he planning for the big day, Annabelle?" my mother asked in rapt anticipation.

"What big day, Mother? You mean our one-year anniversary?" I replied, pretending that I had forgotten it was drawing near (spoiler alert: I hadn't).

"Oh, dare I say your one-year ANNIEversary!" she quipped. She was clearly very proud of herself with that one. "I can only imagine he is planning something very big. Very big indeed. Hopefully as big as an engagement ring!" She could barely contain her delight.

"Oh, I don't know about all that, Mom. I mean, I am only barely 24 years old. I haven't even figured out my career yet. I don't have my own health insurance. I am basically a woman-child. Jeffy is almost 30. He is set on a career path, and I may be more of an obstacle than an asset at this point."

Oh, nonsense. He absolutely *adores* you, Annabelle. He is the one. I can just feel it." She was always having feelings about things. As much as I wanted to believe her and believe that Jefferson was the *one,* I had to remember her feelings about Quinton. And Nash. And Kevin, the booger-eater! Nope. Her feelings could not be trusted.

Although, as much as I didn't want to allow my hopes to exceed my expectations, I have to admit, I was hopeful. Although there were certain little issues that might be considered red flags, I pushed them away and tried to convince myself that my mom was right. He was the one, and we were meant to be. I mean, who cares that I didn't see him every weekend? He had lots of work events and out of town meetings. And why should I worry that we always seemed to hang out at my itty-bitty apartment that I shared with Sophie when he had a large condo all to himself? And, who needed to meet his friends anyway!? Nothing to worry about, I'm sure.

Or, actually, I guess I should have worried.

Chapter 9: Betrayal

I will never forget that fateful day. I had gotten out of work early, and I decided to surprise him. It was a Friday afternoon, and I knew that he and the guys from his firm would often frequent a swanky little bar across the street from their office. "We like to take Friday night to blow off steam, Annie," he would explain. It all seemed perfectly normal. I had to work Friday nights anyway (I honestly couldn't afford to miss out on tips from Friday night dinners), so what did I care if he practiced a little "male bonding" while I worked?

Midway through my shift on this particular Friday evening, a toilet in the women's restroom at *Sunshine Grill* overflowed, and the plumbers couldn't get it to stop. Much to the chagrin of all parties concerned (the manager, Mike, who had to close the place, the workers who would miss out on the Friday night pay, and the customers who had to leave their seats, mid-meal, due to the horrendous smell), everyone was sent packing.

No worries, I thought. *I will turn these veritable lemons into lemonade. I will go home, get dressed up in my fanciest attire, and surprise Jefferson at the bar. He will be thrilled to see me and will relish in the opportunity to show me off to his friends and colleagues.*

I raced home and threw on the little black dress he bought for me a couple of weeks prior while we were out and about on a little shopping jaunt. When he bought me that dress, I secretly wondered when I would ever wear it. I assumed I might wear it out one night for a nice dinner with Jeffy, but I figured that this surprise tryst was even better. What more could he want than for me to show up unannounced and surprise him while wearing it? I found some shoes that would do, and I jumped in the car and headed towards the beach.

Traffic was mediocre, but parking, as usual, was a nightmare. They only had one option at this place, valet. There was no way in hell I was going to use that service. For one thing, it was $10. That was the equivalent of one or two tables of waitressing service. No way was I going to part with that kind of scratch just to avoid a few extra steps. For another thing, I was too embarrassed to pull my beat-up little 1988, baby blue, Nissan Pulsar into the valet line. Forget it, I would walk.

Luckily, I finally found an open spot a few blocks down the street, right next to the little beach shack that rented boogie boards and beach cruisers. I had to parallel park, but my car was fortunately rather small, and I was able to squeeze it into the space fairly quickly.

I strode down Pacific Coast Highway, feet already aching in the heels that were far too high to be precariously walking along a busy thoroughfare, and finally arrived at my destination. Luckily, it was still early, so the place wasn't too crowded, and I could nab a good seat at the bar.

I ordered myself a cocktail and sank into my chair, glad to be off my feet and excited to surprise Jeffy with my presence. As I waited, a beautiful young woman with long black hair and an elegant evening dress walked up and asked if she could sit next to me.

"Of course," I said, happy to oblige this fellow female with the unoccupied seat next to me. Much better than to have to ward off some creepy, half-drunk man looking to hook up with someone. "I am just waiting for my boyfriend to arrive."

"Perfect! So am I," she replied, and she settled into the leather barstool next to me.

"May I order us a drink as we wait for our men?" she asked with a wink.

"Oh, I already ordered mine, but please go ahead. We can drink while we wait." I was struck by this woman's beauty as well as her quiet confidence.

The waitress brought our cocktails, and we sat and shared pleasantries. She mentioned that she was new to this coastal area, having moved here from a neighboring city just a few miles inland. Unlike me, she was clearly comfortable in this sophisticated bar, and she offered that she came here often.

At one point in the conversation, she noticed my Tiffany bracelet and commented that I have great taste. I replied that it was a gift from my boyfriend, and she laughed and showed me her wrist. Identical charm bracelets. We chuckled and remarked about how small the world was.

Little did I know just how small.

The woman mentioned that she and her boyfriend came here every Friday night before they made their way back to his place where they rounded out their evening on the deck of his condo, watching the waves crash in the moonlight.

"That sounds romantic."

"Oh, it is. It gives me something to look forward to after a long week at the office."

I smiled and nodded, suggesting that I understood and was probably in the same position. I didn't really want to blurt out, "Oh, lovely. I usually spend my Friday nights juggling plates of chili fries and hot wings, and refilling all-you-can-drink sodas."

Despite the fact that we obviously had two very different lifestyles, I was happy for this friendly woman and was sure she deserved any good fortune she may be experiencing. *Besides,* I thought to myself, *she may have a fancy office job, but I have Jefferson.*

After maybe 30 minutes of pleasant and easy conversation, I noticed Jefferson walk through the entrance. He was handsome, as usual. He wore the fitted, dark grey suit that I absolutely adored, and it made my heart skip a beat to think about the surprise I was about to deliver. As per usual, he had his face buried in his Nokia, his latest and greatest gadget, so didn't look up to scan the room.

He is going to be so surprised when he sees me.

Suddenly, and without hesitation, the woman next to me jumped up and quickly said "Oh! My boyfriend is here. Nice talking to you!" and scurried along her way. I was curious to see the man she was dating, so I watched her walk up to her boyfriend and throw her arms around him. He embraced her passionately and planted a long, seductive kiss on her neck. It truly was a captivating and alluring moment. The only problem was, it was Jefferson.

***

For what seemed like an eternity, I watched the two of them hug and canoodle and whisper. They were completely and totally in their own world. They made their way to a small booth tucked away in the corner of the room, next to a beautiful window that faced the shore, and they continued their private and clearly intimate conversation.

I marveled at the way in which she effortlessly yet knowingly touched his hand as he spoke, and I was equally blown away by the way his eyes sparkled as his mouth grew to an enormous grin as she replied. I pondered how many times they had met at this place. She had mentioned that this was a weekly routine. More than anything, I wondered how long they had been together.

I wasn't sure how much time passed as I sat there on that barstool. I felt cold and numb. The only sound I could hear was the thumping of my heart in my own ears. I felt like water was rushing all over my body, covering me from head to toe, like I was drowning right there in plain view. I considered for a moment that I had perhaps been the victim of a brain aneurism or maybe even a devastating bomb blast. Everything in my view was fuzzy, and I was so disoriented that I thought I might faint.

"So, this is what death feels like," I heard myself say, to no one.

Despite my better judgment, I decided to forgo what was left of my dignity and walk over to their table. Feeling someone approach, on instinct, they looked up and saw me standing there. The woman, smiling pleasantly, gesturing to Jefferson, said, "Oh hello! Nice to see you again. This is my boyfriend, Jefe." I looked him dead in the eyes and blurted out the three little words that immediately came to mind: "Go fuck yourself."

At this point, chaos ensued. Jeffy began stammering all over the place, saying super original things like "Oh! Annie! Hey! What's up? What are you doing here?!" Meanwhile, this other woman looked shocked, mouth agape, wondering why I just told off her boyfriend.

"What the hell is going on?" she demanded.

"Put it this way," I yelled, "We have the same boyfriend." I gave him one more glare, and then I stormed out of the bar.

I walked without stopping out the front door and down to the end of the driveway to where the sidewalk met the street. Although I was trembling, the adrenaline of the moment propelled me steadily forward. I imagined Jefferson would be running after me at this point, pleading with me to understand that this was all just a big misunderstanding and begging me to give him another chance. In my mind, I was calculating all of the possible things to say to him in reply. Ridiculously basic phrases like *How could you*? and *Why did you do this to me*? and *What the fuck is going on?* came to mind. I was calculating the pros and cons of each response, as I turned to face this undoubtedly ashamed and regretful man head on.

The only problem was he wasn't there. Instead, I could see him through the window, still inside the establishment, clearly pleading with this other woman to understand that it was all just a big misunderstanding and begging her to please forgive him.

Oh my God, I thought, as my stomach fell, and my knees began to buckle. *He chose her.*

***

I don't remember walking to my car, and I don't even remember driving home. All I remember was flailing onto my bed in a heap of tears and mascara, sobbing breathlessly into my pillow and simultaneously screaming expletives at the top of my lungs.

"What the fuck just happened? How could he fucking do this? What the fuck is going on?" I was yelling in between great sobs and helpless moans.

Sophie came running to my rescue. "Oh my God, Annie," she shrieked with a mixture of fear and concern, "What happened?" She rushed over to my bed and quickly wrapped me up in a tender embrace.

"He was (gasp) there (gasp) with someone (gasp) else!" I managed to belt out. All I could do was bury my head in Sophie's lap and allow her to stroke my back and tell me it was going to be alright.

"What?" she asked with shock and confusion. "Jefferson? Did you see Jefferson with another woman?" Sophie was sincerely dismayed.

"Yes!" I cried. "Yes, I did! I went to surprise him, but instead he surprised me!"

"What the hell!? I can't believe he is cheating on you, Annie," she said with sincere bewilderment.

"Actually, Sophie," I replied, choking back my tears, "from what I could tell, I think he was cheating on someone else with me."

I continued to relay the entire humiliating story to Sophie, stopping occasionally to cry, whimper, and wipe my nose.

Sophie became more furious with every detail. "Fuck that guy, Annie. I had a gut feeling that he was an asshat. Something told me he was a player. I fucking knew it. I swear to God, Annie… I will hunt him down… I will grab him by his itty-bitty balls, and I will hang him upside down from a tree. I will gut him with a rusty knife, and I will use his pathetic face like a pinata!" She was really on a roll.

I started to quietly laugh despite myself, thinking of Sophie going on a violent rampage, and I sank further into her arms. Everything seemed to feel better when I was there, wrapped in Sophie's embrace. I slowly started to calm down, and eventually I sat up and looked at her.

"He didn't choose me, Soph," I said with a whimper. "Just like Marshall. He didn't choose me."

"It's okay, Ann," she said with a sweetness and softness in her voice that I sincerely appreciated. "I know it stings, but I promise it will be okay. It's his loss, Annabelle. Not yours. He doesn't deserve you. He obviously never did."

I wasn't sure I believed her, but I decided not to argue. Over the many years I had known her, I had learned that it was usually unwise to argue with her, especially concerning matters of the heart.

"Well, fine then," I replied, basically unconvinced but also zapped of all energy and incapable of disagreeing. "It just hurts, Soph. It hurts so much."

Sophie let out a long, slow exhale. She tenderly grabbed ahold of my hands, and she focused her gaze directly upon me. I could tell she had something important to say, but I also sensed something else. Was there apprehension in her eyes?

"Listen to me, Annabelle," she said sternly, but with sincerity in her voice, "and listen up good. Jefferson does not deserve you. He was lucky to date you. Hell, he was lucky to even fucking know you." She squeezed my hands for emphasis, and I could feel her body slightly trembling beneath her grip. She looked away, seemingly unprepared to continue this line of discussion. What was she holding back?

Tears started to well in her eyes, but she cleared her throat and looked back at me squarely. She continued, "You are precious, Annabelle, and you are spectacular. If Jefferson can't see that, then he is truly a fool."

Sophie looked away again, as I could sense the agitation in her voice. My pulse suddenly started to accelerate, and I felt a tingling sensation race up and down my body.

"I love you, Annie," she said quickly, and then she abruptly let go of my hands. She stood up and walked out of my bedroom. She paused for a moment in the doorway, turned toward me, and repeated, "He is an absolute fool," and then she turned around again and left my room.

As I sat there on my bed, suddenly alone, I felt an ache deep within me that I hadn't sensed previously. What was this sensation I was experiencing? Was it disappointment? Was it longing? Was it regret?

I sat there for a few moments, considering this confusing state, and wondering if this feeling would ever be identified. I quietly wept and moaned for what seemed like an eternity, until I finally sank deeper into my bed and tried to fall asleep.

All that was running through my mind were two questions playing on an interminable loop: *Why didn't he didn't choose me*? and *What is this feeling?* I tossed and turned, trying to rid my mind of these uncomfortable and confusing questions, but they were playing on repeat for what seemed like forever. After some time, however, I finally fell into a restless sleep. That night, I had a strange and curious dream. I dreamed I was standing on a crowded beach and a giant wave was about to make landfall. I watched it barreling toward the shore. It was sure to obliterate everything in its path, but I was simply frozen in place. There was chaos all around me, with people running every which way and screaming at me to move. "It's coming!" they cried, "Run for your life!" However, I just stood there, immobile, unable to break away... unable to even close my eyes. I watched the wave make its way steadily toward the shore, toward me. I braced for certain impact, convinced that it would sweep me away at any moment. Except, instead of crashing into me with the force of a tidal wave, knocking me into a house or a car or another person, obliterating me with its force and sheer velocity, it suddenly became Sophie's arms, sweetly, gently, and lovingly stroking my hair back and looking me right in the eyes and saying: *I see you, and I choose you.*

Chapter 10: Rebound

When the dust of that fateful Friday night settled, things eventually started to go back to normal. Despite the fact that my heart had been shattered, this wasn't my first rodeo. I had walked the path of heartbreak before, and I knew where it led. I finally came to realize that what I needed in this moment was a rebound man. Hot off the Jefferson disaster, my confidence was at an all-time low. I needed to regain some of the mojo I lost, along with my pride, back at that swanky bar next to the beach.

"Relax, Ann," Sophie said. "You just need a slump buster. Give it some time, and you will find someone."

"Soph, this is getting critical. If I don't find a guy to date soon, I think I may have to just call it a day and join a monastery."

"I think you mean a convent. Unless you are looking to convert a monk?" Sophie asked smugly, with a chuckle and fabricated curiosity.

"Convert a monk?" I replied with a chuckle, "I can't even seem to find an eligible bachelor out in the wild. I certainly don't think I would have any luck with a monk!" I sarcastically hung my head in defeat.

"You will find someone, Annie, " Sophie replied with cool confidence. "Just trust in the process."

"How do you remain so positive, Soph? And, also, what the hell is this elusive process you are always talking about?"

"I stay positive because I am too damn busy to dwell on whether or not I am going to find my soulmate. Law school is no joke, Ann" she said as she dramatically thumbed through pages and pages of legal articles. "And the process, my dear Annabelle, is the law of attraction. Like attracts like. Put out that good juju that you will find a man, and a man will surely come a runnin'."

"Figures that a law student would believe in the *law of attraction*. Is there any such thing as the *law of I just want to find a man who isn't a complete douchebag, so let me point to him and then you can bring him to me oh sovereign gods of the dating universe*?" I pleaded in half-jest.

"Sure, Ann. It's called Match.com."

Damn! I thought. *She has an answer for everything*. "What the hell is that?"

"You haven't heard of it? It's the latest and greatest technology to hit the world wide web. You just make a profile on the internet and send it out to thousands if not millions of people who are also on their website. You list all the things you want in a life partner, and bing, bang, boom… they match you up with your one true love. It honestly seems foolproof." She was so eager and optimistic, she sounded like she might be on their payroll.

"Oh my God, Sophie. That sounds totally creepy!" I quipped. "How do I sign up?" I said with a laugh.

So, there it was. I was at the point in my life where I was no longer able to find a suitable partner just out in the world on my own. I apparently needed a computer to find one for me. If I wasn't so frantic to find my prince, I would have been more leery. This new invention called *the internet* was an elusive and frightening place as far as I was concerned. Nonetheless, I listened to Sophie's sage advice, took the leap of faith, and dove headfirst into the unchartered sea of online dating.

***

The first thing I did was buy a cheap computer. Sophie and I had one in our apartment, but we had to share it. Since she was much busier than I was, with arguably much more important work (though, can one *really* say with certainty that completing law school assignments is more important than finding one's prince?), she got dibs.

Although I was making more money these days, extra spending cash was not limitless. I had been promoted to assistant manager of *Sunshine Grill,* and I was also moonlighting as a copywriter for a new apartment rental firm that had just launched on the world wide web. They paid me $25 per page for copy describing the available apartments. The work was a bit mind numbing (I mean, there are only so many ways to say that an apartment is clean and offers good, natural light), but it was fairly easy work, and the extra money certainly helped.

I had been saving up to buy a new car, since I was currently driving my late grandfather's old Buick. My

Nissan Pulsar had finally bit the dust, so my mother gave me the car she had inherited when her father passed. It had no air conditioning, the front passenger seat was indefinitely stuck in a reclined position, and the radio only played AM stations. Nonetheless, this dating crisis of mine seemed to be even more pressing. I needed a computer so that I could find a man. It was as simple as that.

"Kill two birds with one stone, Annabelle," my mother would say. "All you need to do is find a man with a good, solid income, and he can buy you a new car." Her logic, she reasoned, was flawless.

"First of all, I don't know why you would mention killing birds, mother. That seems extreme," I said, as she exhaled loudly and reminded me that it was simply a figure of speech. "However," I continued, "I can buy my own car. I just need a computer to hire that robot matchmaker to find a man for me. It's a new age, Mom. Welcome to the future!" I was trying to convince both of us that this was a good idea.

"You know, I don't trust the world wide web," she replied. "Who knows what kind of lunatics may be lying in wait for a lovely young woman to come along. Besides, dear, don't you think it makes you look a little desperate?"

"I am desperate, Mom!" I said with exasperation.

Apparently, she had no rebuttal, so the case was closed. I was desperate, and I needed to contract the robot cupid ASAP.

***

"Ok, first order of business..." Sophie declared as she took out the shoe box from the hall closet that held our favorite photographs, "We need to find the perfect profile picture of you."

"Ugh. I didn't think about that. I guess I do need a profile picture, don't I? I am not sure too many men would be interested in going out on a date with a woman, sight unseen."

"Truth," she said.

"How about this one?" I asked, as I held up a ridiculous photo of me when I had gotten snow burned the past spring during a ski trip to the local mountains. My face was beet red, my eyes were nearly swollen shut, and my lips were engorged to about 5 times their normal size. "Maybe he will feel sorry for me, or perhaps he will refer me to his single dermatologist friend for a check-up?" I said with a smile and a chuckle.

"Oh my God, Annie. You're puffy as fuck! Hell to the no! I know you're kidding, but damn, girl. Just no!" Sophie wasn't appreciating my attempts at levity. "Come on, now. This is serious business. We need to find the right photo that says, 'I am a hot piece of ass, but I am also a respectable woman.'"

"Well, that's a tall order, Soph. That may be a pretty difficult balance to strike." I was starting to worry that this might be a futile project.

I rummaged through the shoebox for a few minutes, and I came up with one I thought may have potential.

"How about this one?" I asked in earnest, holding up a photo of me at her family's lake house the previous summer. I was sunbathing on the beach, lounging in a tasteful two-piece bikini, reading an Anaïs Nin book.

"Close!" she blurted, "But, it needs to show your face more. The last thing you want is to be considered a butterface."

"A butterface? What the hell is a butterface?" I asked, clearly in a state of deep confusion.

"You know, Annie," she replied, "it's like when someone says 'she is gorgeous everywhere but her face.... but her face... butterface! Get it?" She never ceased to amaze me with her knowledge of the juvenile vernacular.

"Wow, Soph. Gross." I said with sincere disdain in my voice.

"I know, I know," she conceded, "but, we need to think like the average man here. We can't just select a mediocre photo and call it a day. Also," she continued, "who knows if any potential suitor will even know who Anaïs Nin is!?"

"Ok, fine, fair question. Although," I argued, "do I really want to date a man who doesn't know who she is?" I sighed, thinking that she was probably right and that I needed to temper my expectations here. "Ok," I relented, "maybe I need to take a new photo. I am not sure I will be able to find a picture that demonstrates all of my 'desirable qualities' among the photos I already have."

Sophie agreed that taking a new photo was probably best, so we took a whole afternoon to create the perfect picture. Let's just say it involved numerous costume changes, props, backdrops, hairstyles, cosmetic products, and facial expressions. We finally landed on the right combination of sexy and wholesome, and we sent it to print. It was a photo of me, in a red, flowy mini dress, standing amid a field of yellow wildflowers. I was daintily holding one of the flowers next to my chest, with my head bent ever-so-slightly downward, with my eyes looking up toward the camera. I had a knowing smile that Sophie said made me look "wholesome, yet horny." I guess that was a good thing… So, there it was: my Match.com profile pic. "The money shot," Sophie called it. I was ready to hit the world wide web. Sophie couldn't have been more proud.

***

As soon as I uploaded my profile, I immediately regretted it. I had to include all sorts of personal information about myself in order for the robot to find my "perfect match." It felt incredibly invasive. This was no less daunting a task than taking the damn photo. Did I sound too needy? Did I look too horny? It was all so confusing. And scary. And intimidating.

I said, "What if I get a bunch of creepers winking at me, Soph?" I suddenly had another thought and gasped, "What if I don't get any winks at all?" I was itching to remove my profile. Hell, burn the computer to the ground at this point.

"Just relax, Ann. You look amazing. Your answers are impeccable. The men will be banging down your virtual door in no time. Besides, you get to pick who you want to meet too, Annie. This is the 1990s. You don't have to wait around to be asked on a date like some 1950s girl at a sock hop!"

"Ok, you're right" I conceded. "I have some control over this situation, so I will just see what happens." I tried to relax and channel some of Sophie's Zen energy.

"There you go, Annie," Sophie agreed with a smile, "I think you are going to be just fine."

And so, I waited. The first few interactions were lackluster at best. Many of the men who initially seemed like they had potential quickly fizzled out once I had an opportunity to talk to them on the phone. I mean, how could I take someone seriously who bragged that he had "never read a book in his life"? One guy even admitted to feeding his pet lizard a grasshopper which he held between his own teeth on a dare. Honestly. Who does that? Not to mention, who shares that kind of information on a pre-date? No. Just no.

I was starting to feel hopeless and discouraged, but then I had a surprising match come my way. His name was Marcus, and he seemed nice enough. He was a very handsome man, in his late 20s, and he was gainfully employed. Good start. We spoke on the phone, and he didn't say anything too shocking or too creepy. There was no grasshopper or lizard talk, and nothing got my spidey senses tingling. So, I agreed to meet him for pizza on the following Saturday afternoon.

"Sophie!" I burst out as she walked through the door that evening, "I did it! I got a date! Well, or should I say, the computer got me a date!"

"Nice! Way to go, Ann. I told you it was just a numbers game. Go through enough profiles, and one is bound to work out." Sophie looked at everything so pragmatically.

I was beginning to feel like this could really work for me. *Take advantage of the technology of today,* I would tell myself. *All I needed was an algorithm to find my Prince Charming! Who knew!?*

***

The fateful day arrived, and I was a ball of nerves as I tried to get ready. It was like I had never been on a date before. I was jittery and uneasy. I felt like I was going to vomit or maybe even pass out. Thankfully, Sophie was there to calm me down and keep me grounded.

I tried on a dozen different outfits. Nothing looked right. I suddenly felt bloated in all the wrong places. Should I wear a dress? That seemed too fancy for a pizza place. Should I wear ripped jeans and some flip-flops? Ugh. That may look too casual. After much debate, we landed on one outfit that we both agreed would work. We settled on black jeans, an off-the-shoulder grey sweater, and flats. I arranged my hair in soft waves around my face, and I applied what I considered to be a tasteful amount of makeup.

"He is one lucky bastard, Annie." She told me, with great sass in her voice, "Go in there with confidence and remember that he just won the dating lottery." She sincerely was the greatest hype-man (or, hype-woman as it were) of all time.

I tried to own that sense of certainty and self-confidence, and I left the house feeling positive and optimistic about the date.

As I entered the restaurant, I spotted him immediately. His appearance held up to his profile photo (something, I came to find out later, that was not always the case), and I slid confidently into the booth across from him.

"Hi! I'm Annie," I said, trying to strike that balance between upbeat and happy but not over-anxious or nervous.

"Oh, hey! I'm Marcus. Obviously," he said with a bit of regret, it appeared, at the stating of the obvious. "Nice to finally meet you in person!"

He offered a broad smile and told me I looked nice.

"Thanks, Marcus. You too," I said, awkwardly. Wanting to change the subject, I quickly offered, "Have you eaten here before?"

"Oh, no, I haven't," he replied. "but my brother ate here last week and said the pizzas are really good. I guess they specialize in pizzas from some certain region in Italy where it only takes a minute or two to cook."

"Oh!" I replied, "That's cool. Maybe they make the pizzas in a brick oven like they do in Naples."

"Yeah, maybe. I hope they live up to my brother's hype."

We engaged in some pleasant small talk as the waitress approached. She asked if we were ready to order, and I nodded yes. Marcus said he was also ready, so he asked me to please go first.

So far, so good, I thought to myself.

"Sure, thanks," I said, as I looked toward the waitress. "I think I will just have the margarita pizza. It's basic, I know, but it has always been one of my favorites. Who doesn't love some tomato and basil?" I wasn't sure why I was suddenly adding extra and unnecessary commentary. I chalked it up to nerves.

"You got it," she replied, seemingly unfazed by my random observations. "It is a house specialty," she added. Then, she looked to Marcus and asked, "what would you like, sir?"

"I will have this one," he said as he pointed to the menu. "I can't pronounce these Italian words too good."

Too *good*? I thought to myself. Huh. *Ok, I will give him a break here,* I thought. Maybe he was nervous, and he just slipped up a bit and meant to say "well" instead of "good." I always like to give people the benefit of the doubt.

However, I couldn't help but to peek over onto the menu to see which Italian word really stumped him so badly that he resorted to pointing.

Oh dear, I thought. *This isn't good.*

BOURGEOISIE. The pizza's name was bourgeoisie.

Needless to say, this was our first and last date.

***

"I can't believe you dumped him just because he didn't know how to pronounce bourgeoisie, Annie! It is a difficult word after all," Sophie sighed as she exaggeratedly rolled her eyes.

"It's not just because he couldn't pronounce it, Soph. He also thought it was an Italian word! I rest my case." (Side note: I have always enjoyed using legalese when talking to Sophie.)

"You should give him another chance, Annie," she pleaded.

"Objection!" I yelled.

"Sustained," she relented with a sigh.

"I am beginning to feel like this whole thing is ill-fated, Soph," I lamented. "Maybe I should just cancel my Match.com subscription and adopt a cat."

"Absolutely not, Annabelle." Sophie found renewed energy. "I need you to get back on that horse and ride it 'til you find your pardner," she said with a chuckle. "See what I did there, Ann?" she asked, obviously proud of herself for delivering this clever word play.

"Yes, yes. Very cute, Soph." I said half-heartedly. "Ok, I will give it one more month. That's it, though. ONE MONTH. That is all I can take. If nothing pans out in that time, I am investing in the spinster starter kit."

"Fine, fine," she agreed. "One more month. Just keep the faith, Ann. I have a good feeling that you will find the man of your dreams."

And so it went. I continued to field mediocre man after mediocre man. I was talking to one guy for a couple of weeks who I thought may have potential. He was a personal trainer and life coach. He worked at a fitness club near our apartment, and he was able to score me a free, unlimited use day pass to his gym. I was looking forward to getting into better shape myself, and I thought this might be the perfect situation for me. Although, I did find it odd that for a personal trainer and life coach, he looked uncharacteristically sluggish all of the time. *Eh, who knows,* I thought to myself. I chalked it up to working too much. I must admit, his physique was impeccable, and he seemed to have a good handle on his life affairs. Turns out, his life affairs were not the only affairs in his life. I serendipitously found out that he was sleeping with no fewer than five or six of his clients. As disappointing as it was, at least I got to keep the unlimited day pass. And no wonder he had trouble with his stamina. He was working overtime!

Just as the month was nearing its close, and hope was beginning to fade, I opened the computer one more time. *Hope springs eternal,* I thought to myself, as I opened my Match.com page. I half suspected that this would be my last attempt at online dating. Nothing had panned out, and checking the inbox was actually becoming a bit of a chore. But to my surprise and delight, I opened my computer to find a devilishly handsome man smiling right at me. *Hello, Gorgeous!* Introducing, Chip.

Chapter 11: Chip

There he was, looking right at me through my computer screen. He had dark, wavy hair, almond-shaped brown eyes, and a 5000-watt smile that could land a plane. His name was Alfonso, but, according to his profile page, he was an avid golfer and preferred go by his golf-inspired nickname: Chip. He lived in town, and, apparently, he attended our rival high school. From what I could tell, he went to college out of state but, like Sophie and me, he found his way back to suburban Southern California life in our hometown post-graduation.

After a couple of weeks of casual phone calls and flirtatious banter via a handy new form of communication called the text message, we decided to meet for a drink. I could tell that Chip had an excellent personality. He was exuberant and fun-loving, and his laugh was absolutely infectious. I was anxious to meet him in person. There was a hip, new bar and nightclub not far from my apartment, and we planned to meet there after work on Thursday night. I thought a weekend night would be better, but he said he had an early tee-time on Saturday morning, so he preferred to meet on Thursday.

Oh, well. I don't have to work on Friday anyway, I thought. I suspected the bar may be less crowded on a weekday night anyway, and it might make for an easier opportunity to talk and get to know him better. I was all in.

As the date approached, I began to get jittery with eager anticipation. I remember telling Sophie that if he danced as well as he flirted, I would be in for a real treat. Sophie remarked that although he was objectively gorgeous, I needed to remember that he was lucky to be on a date with me. Yep, she was always in my corner.

Unfortunately, I struggled to get out of work on time on Thursday. One of my coworkers had called in sick, and another one was out on maternity leave. I finally got out of there more than an hour later than I should have, so I was in a rush the entire way home. I am lucky I didn't get pulled over for speeding; that would have really put a damper in my already stressful drive. I had to swing by my apartment after work to change my clothes and freshen up a bit. I originally planned to have a couple hours to get ready, but now I was in a mad dash to even make it on time. Unfortunately, I hadn't pre-planned my date outfit, so I had to scramble to make something work. *Where is Sophie when I need her?* I thought to myself. She was working late this evening as well, and I knew she wouldn't be home until well after I was gone. In desperation, I just seized the first outfit I saw in my closet, and I grabbed the cutest high heeled shoes I owned. Unfortunately, due to the delay, I ended up arriving to the bar about 30 minutes later than I had planned.

I'm just fashionably late, I told myself. *I am sure he will be waiting with bated breath,* I thought to myself, although somewhat unconvincingly.

As I entered the bar, I was surprised to find it much busier than I had anticipated. "Wow. It's hoppin' for a Thursday night," I whispered to myself.

The music was loud, and people were scattered all over the dance floor. The energy in the place was intense and frenetic. The crowd was absolutely electric. I waded through dozens of sweaty and breathless people lining the bar, trying to get the poor, lone bartender's attention to buy another drink. I was desperately looking for that gorgeous face I had committed to memory. *Surely, he must be seated at one of these barstools, just waiting for my arrival,* I imagined.

As my eyes scanned the club, looking for what I assumed would be a solo man also scanning the room looking for me, I heard a large group of people begin to chant on the dancefloor.

What in the world are they saying? I thought to myself.

As I focused intently, I began to make sense of the rhythmic mantra.

"Chip! Chip! Chip! Chip! Chip!" I heard them yell.

Are they yelling 'Chip?' I whispered to myself.

I zigzagged my way through the line of thirsty partygoers and hurried to the sea of people on the dancefloor, toward the genesis of that throbbing chant. To my astonishment, I was confronted with the sight of my date for the evening, dead center on the dancefloor. He was positioned in a near back bend, with a large-breasted and scantily clad woman rhythmically pouring Patron down his throat while the crowd cheered him on. As he took what appeared to be the last swig, he bolted upright, both hands above his head, and shouted "hell yeah!" as he made finger pistols toward the ceiling.

The crowd replied in a collective "YEAHHHHH!," and he slowly pivoted toward the bar. Amid the chaos of the moment, his eyes somehow caught mine. For the briefest second, I wondered if he would even recognize me from my picture. Hell, at this point, would he even remember that we were set to meet? Within a mere moment, however, his eyes lit up, he cracked a giant smile, and he shrieked, "Hey gorgeous! You're finally here!"

I had an impulse to look behind me to see if he was talking to someone else, but within a second, he was right up on me, sweeping me into his arms and literally off of my feet, twirling me in a circle, embraced in a bear hug that lasted longer than I suspected it would.

As he set my back down, he took a half step back and cried, "Damn girl! You look fine tonight!" "Come on!" he yelled, and he pulled me onto the dancefloor.

To say that I didn't have fun would be a bold-faced lie. We danced and drank and sang our favorite songs at the top of our lungs for hours. All the while, I admit that I was thinking, *what exactly is happening here? Are we on a date, or are we both just attendees at this dance party?*

Just as I was about to expire from sheer exhaustion, Chip reached for my hand and said, "Let's go grab a seat at the bar."

Part of me was thankful, as I was tired, and I wanted to sit down. However, the other part of me was skeptical that we would ever find a seat, as this place was packed, and it didn't seem to be easing up any as the night wound down.

"Over here!" I heard a couple of men yell.

Chip twirled me around and marched us toward the sound of his buddies, holding seats for us.

Chip introduced me to his friends, one by one. "This goofy guy on my left is Barry. The tall, skinny one in the shades is David. We call him Davey McFatFuck just to bust his balls. The crazy-looking dude in the cheetah print pants is James. And this," pointing to the gentleman who snuck up behind us, "is Creeper. He is always just appearing out of nowhere."

"My guys," he cried, "this is the lovely lady I told you about. This is Annabelle."

We spent the rest of the evening at the bar, laughing, drinking, and basically enjoying one another's company. The guys all took turns recounting funny anecdotes about Chip, and I rather enjoyed hearing the inside scoop about this man I was meeting in person for the first time.

One of my favorite anecdotes was a story dating back to high school. Apparently, Chip had attended the *other* Christian school in our hometown. We used to play them in football, and I wondered if I ever saw him at a game. I was a cheerleader, after all, and he was on the football squad. In any event, his friends told the story of how one time, after a particularly grueling football practice in the Southern California heat, Chip was wiped out at the end of it. Protocol at his school was to leave the practice field and head into the locker room on the far side of the school property. From there, they would change out of their pads and uniforms, take a shower, redress in their normal, street clothes, pack their pads, helmet, and uniform into their enormous and heavy duffle bags, and walk all the way back across campus to the parking lots where their cars awaited them. On this one particular afternoon, however, Chip was feeling extremely tired (*and lazy,* he added), so he decided he didn't want to make the long walk to and from the locker room. Instead, he would duck into the side door of the gymnasium and do a quick change there and head straight to his car. He would save a lot of time and extra steps, and he figured he would be in and out of the gym in a mere blink of an eye. He remembered that the basketball team was at an away game that day, so he knew the gym would be empty. *No harm, no foul,* he admitted.

"But this is where things went very wrong, very quickly" Davey McFatFuck chimed.

Barry continued, "So there he was, thinking he was totally alone in the gym. He would do a quick costume change, and all would be fine. Unfortunately for young Chip, here, just as he removed his football pants, in walks the principal, Ms. Jones (he put an emphasis on *Ms.*), leading a campus tour to some prospective parents."

"I can just hear her now," James interrupted. In an exaggerated high, female-sounding voice, he began, "And this, dear, prospective family, is the gym where our student athletes praise Jesus with their talents on the basketball court."

"Yeah!" Barry laughed. "Imagine their surprise when they saw our very own Chip, standing there in nothing but his tube socks, looking like a deer in headlights!"

"Praise Jesus is right," interrupted Chip. "In my defense, Ms. Jones looked me up and down for a good 5-10 seconds before she realized the predicament she was in and rushed this poor family out the door!"

"Oh my God, dude," Davey chimed, "Do you honestly believe Ms. Jones was giving you the eye?"

"Hell yeah, she was. Every time I saw her after that day, she got as red as a lobster and did an abrupt about-face!" Chip insisted. "I'm telling you, my dudes, she was into me!"

The five of us were laughing until we cried at the thought of poor Ms. Jones having to explain to this fine family that no, our students are not typically naked in the gymnasium.

By the time the bar was closing, I was utterly wiped out. My feet hurt from dancing (I definitely wore the wrong shoes), and my cheeks hurt from laughing. I found Chip's confidence and carefree attitude to be intoxicating, and I hoped that he would want to see me again.

We made our way to the exit at the end of the night, and I said goodbye to his buddies.

"Cool meeting you, Annie," yelled James.

"You too!" I replied and waved at them as they made their way to their cars.

"Where are you parked?" Chip asked.

"Right over there," I said, motioning to the far north end of the lot.

"Alrighty then," he replied, and he grabbed my hand and walked me to my car. When we arrived, he let go and asked if I was okay to drive.

I assured him that I was.

"Can I call you tomorrow"? he asked.

"Sure," I replied, attempting to hide my excitement, "sounds good."

At this point, I wondered what to do next. Should I thank him for a lovely evening? Should I extend my hand and shake it as though we had just completed a lucrative business deal? Should I go in for a respectable side hug?

As I weighed my numerous options, he interrupted my contemplation, wrapped his arm around my waist, pulled me in close to him, and kissed me. It was a sweet kiss… firm, but gentle. Tasteful, but not rushed. I felt a tingling sensation run from my lips all the way down to my toes and back up again.

He let go of my waist, took a step back, held onto my hands, and beamed that enormous smile. He looked me dead in the eyes for what felt like a lifetime but was probably only about 5-10 seconds. I felt a little weak in the knees as I stared back into those stunning brown eyes, and it was all I could do to remember to breathe. Finally, he spoke: "Great! Talk to you then." He squeezed my hands before he let them go, and he opened my car door and motioned for me to get in. I slid into the driver's seat, and he closed the door. He looked at me for a moment, winked, and strode off towards the other side of the parking lot, presumably to his car.

***

I woke up the next morning, feet still sore from dancing in high heels all night, but on cloud nine from the fun and exhilarating night I had just experienced.

I couldn't wait to tell Sophie all about it, so I quickly ran into her room to share the news.

"Where is she?" I uttered aloud.

I looked at the clock and realized it was almost 10 a.m. Sophie had been at work for more than an hour. I made my way to the kitchen to make myself some coffee and a piece of toast, and I saw a note from her on the counter.

It read: *"I heard you chanting Chip! Chip! Chip! Chip! As you waked in the door last night. Sounds like you had a good date! Can't wait to hear all about it. Talk to you later tonight. XXOO, Soph"*

I spent the entire day recounting the night before and eagerly anticipating his call. *Should I answer on the first ring?* I wondered. *No, that's too needy,* I decided. *Should I let it go to voicemail?* I considered the pros and cons. *No,* I reasoned, *I don't want to be too aloof.*

I decided I would split the difference and answer it on a cool, ring number three.

Next, I considered what I wanted to talk about. He was such an energetic, fun-loving guy. His flirtatious banter was on point, so I needed to match his energy for sure. I considered all of the stories his friends told me the night before, and I found myself laughing out loud as I recalled them. I was anxiously awaiting our next conversation and hoped it would be very soon. I didn't have to work that day, so I spent the entire afternoon just sitting around, anticipating the phone call. Unfortunately, I waited and waited, but no phone call ever came.

When Sophie waked in the door that evening, she found me slumped on the couch, listlessly scrolling through the channels on the TV, not really watching anything.

"Hey!" she said, as she crossed the living room toward the couch, "what are you doing? I thought you would be frolicking around the apartment, all giddy and aflutter!" She seemed genuinely surprised.

"Ugh, nothing" I replied, solemnly. "I have been waiting all day for a phone call, but I guess that's not going to happen." I was unexpectedly crestfallen.

"Oh, relax, Annie." Sophie said as she sat down next me. "You know how guys are. They don't want to seem overeager. I am sure he is just playing it cool."

Maybe, I considered.

Still, I waited anxiously for him to call. When I didn't hear from him for the rest of the night, I figured it would be at least Saturday night or Sunday until I did, as he had a pre-planned golf game scheduled for Saturday morning. As the entire weekend came and went, I began feeling deflated and discouraged. Apparently, the connection I felt wasn't reciprocated. Soon, I became resigned that it was obviously just a one and done, and, despite my disappointment, I decided to move on.

However, just when I believed I had put the whole incident behind me, my phone rang.

Having just purchased new cordless phones from Circuit City with "Caller ID" on them, I saw that Alfonso was calling. It was a Wednesday evening, nearly three weeks after our first and only date.

No way I am going to answer, I told myself.

"Soph!" I screamed at the top of my lungs, "It's him!"

Sophie came tearing out of her room, running straight for me. "Oh my God!" she cried. "I *told* you he would call."

"Should I answer it?" I asked, second guessing my decision to let it go to voicemail.

"Hell no. Let that fuckwit leave a message."

We let it ring until it stopped. We held our breath, waiting for the little red light to come on, indicating that there was a message waiting.

"Oh, damn, Soph. What if he doesn't leave a message?" I asked with trepidation in my voice.

Sophie had all the confidence in the world. "He will."

Each second that passed felt like days. Our gaze was laser-focused on that phone. We were transfixed, waiting to see that little, red light pop on. Finally, it happened. There was a message.

We both jumped at once, eager to play the message back. Before I could hit the "play" button, Sophie stopped me. "Now remember, Annie, he is lucky to even know you. Whatever pathetic excuse he has for ghosting you for the last three weeks is not valid. He needs to earn your affection."

"Yeah, yeah, for sure, Soph." I said absently. "Let's just hear what he has to say." I couldn't wait to push that button.

I started the message playback, and his voice poured out of the tinny speaker. "Hey, Annabelle. It's me, Chip. Hey, listen, I am sorry it's been a minute. I have been super busy with the boys. I'd love to take you out, though. Hit me up when you're available. Peace."

'Huh…" we said in unison.

"It's been a minute?" Sophie repeated. "No, dude, it's been like 30,000 minutes!" I always marveled at her quick math. "And he's *been with the boys*?" she asked. "What boys?" She seemed earnestly perplexed.

"Uh" I stammered, "I guess he means his friends…?" I was about 80% sure that's what he meant. Unless, of course, he has a secret family he forgot to mention.

"Should I call him back?" I asked with sincerity.

"Call him back?" Sophie looked like she was going to blow a gasket, "Absolutely not! He can call you again and we shall see if you are available at that time." She couldn't believe I was considering returning his call.

"Yeah," I said, "I get it… but if I wait to call him back, then he may wait to call me again, and then it may be several more weeks before I see him. I don't want to get caught up in these stupid, childish games."

"Look, call him if you want, but you heard it here first: this is absolute bullshit. He is clearly not taking you seriously, and that is a problem."

I knew in my heart that Sophie was right (let's face it, she usually is), and I told her as much and pledged not to return his call. I sort of meant it at the time, but by the following morning, I gave in and returned it after all. He seemed genuinely happy to hear from me, and not even a little bit abashed for not calling for a couple weeks. I decided not to mention anything about that. I played it cool and went with "Hey, how's it goin'? I got your message. What's up?"

"Oh, sweet. I am glad you called. Yeah, I was wondering if you wanted to go out tonight? Maybe around 6?" he sounded so casual.

Although I thought it might be wise to play a little bit coy, I was pretty excited to see him again, so I decided to just say yes. "Sure, I think I'm free. Should I meet you somewhere specific?"

"I can pick you up," he replied. "I think you said you live off Main. Is that right? I'm not far from there myself."

"Oh!" my heart did a little two-step, "Sure. That would be great. Oh," I threw in as an afterthought, "What should I wear?"

"Something nice," he replied.

Now my heart did a back handspring in my chest.

I gave him my address, and he said he would pick me up at 6 p.m. I knew Sophie would be home by then, and I was a little nervous about that. I would probably have to come clean about calling him this morning. Ugh. But on the upside, she would get to see that million-dollar smile and finally understand what all the hype was about.

Luckily, I only had to work for a few hours in the afternoon, so I had plenty of time to get ready. I washed and dried my hair, tried on a dozen different outfits, and spent an hour perfecting my makeup. I even painted my nails. When Sophie walked in around 5:45, I was just putting on the finishing touches.

One look at me and she rolled her eyes. "Of course you called him…" she said, completely unsurprised.

"Ok, yes. I might have called him back." I said quickly, "But hear me out: he is picking me up and taking me out. You are my best friend, so you are legally required to be happy for me."

"Actually, I'm not sure that's how the law works, Ann" she joked. "But then again, I am only a lawyer, so what would I know about the law anyway?" She sounded half amused, half exasperated.

Nonetheless, in true Sophie fashion, she helped me finalize my outfit, and she seemed sincerely happy that I was happy.

When the doorbell rang, she smiled as she watched me glide across the living room floor, anxious to answer it. I suspect that her smile turned to a grimace, however, as soon as I opened the door and she saw Chip, with four of his best friends in tow behind him.

Turns out, Chip took me to a party at the local golf club. It was me, Chip, and about 50 of Chip's closest acquaintances.

Although I ended up having a decent time, I wondered when I might go on a solo date with him. Turns out, I pretty much figured out the answer to that question: never. I don't think I was ever going to go on a date with him alone. After about a dozen group dates, I realized that he was simply a party-boy who wasn't looking for anything serious. You may be thinking that a dozen is probably about 10 too many group dates to have tolerated before coming to this inevitable conclusion. And you would probably be right. But what can I say? It's intoxicating being with someone like Chip. He is the life of the party, and the party doesn't stop. Well, until it does. I decided that Sophie was indeed right (shocker). He certainly did not prioritize me. So, I decided to prioritize myself. I worked up a big speech that I was going to give him when I told him I no longer wanted to see him. Sadly, though predictably, that speech never came to fruition. He called me one time, but I didn't answer it, and I didn't call him back. I waited him out to see when he would call back again and then I would hit him with my well-rehearsed and savage monologue. As fate would have it, he never did call back. Chip chose his boys. Easiest breakup ever.

Luckily, I never told Mom about Chip. It was already deeply depressing knowing that once again I was not chosen. The only thing that would make it worse would be to have my mother tell me how I let another one get away. So, back to the robot matchmaker I went. Call me a hopeless romantic, but I still remained optimistic that the computer could work its magic. To my delight, it finally did. One fine day, it brought a beautiful man directly into my inbox. Hello, heart, meet Francis.

Chapter 12: Francis

"Now this guy has potential," I called to Sophie, as she walked through the front door.

"Who does?" she asked, setting her purse and keys down on the counter. I could tell she had a long and arduous day, but in true Sophie fashion, she perked up on my behalf. She always showed up for me when I needed her.

"Francis. Look at him, Soph! He has that 'I know what women want' look about him." I was not sure what that look was, specifically, but for some reason, I was sure he had it.

Sophie came sauntering over and peered over my shoulder at the man staring at her from the computer screen. "I am not sure if he knows what women want, Ann, but I can surely see that you want him," she replied.

"Well, he's not ugly, that's for sure! Damn! Look at that jawline. He is fine, Soph! I am gonna give him a wink and see what happens." I was suddenly hopeful again, and it felt good.

***

Luckily for me, Francis winked back, and we spent the next few days getting to know one another over the phone. He was an interesting guy, much less electrifying, perhaps, than Chip… but if there's one thing I knew, it's that I did not need another life-of-the-party man-child.

After a week or more of casual conversation, I agreed to finally meet him at a local coffee shop. There was a new coffee chain in town called Starbucks, and it was all the rage. Apparently, it started in Seattle. Seeing as this was the 1990s and grunge was the coolest scene there was, anything that came from Seattle was considered hip. Nirvana? Yes, please. Pearl Jam? Absolutely. The Mariners? Fuck it, I'll take 'em. After my less-than-optimal experience at the Italian joint that Sophie will forever refer to as "pizzagate," I figured that dinner may be asking too much for a first encounter. Drinks with Chip obviously didn't end the way I wanted them to either, so I decided a quick coffee date would be a better idea. Even if coffee didn't land me a soulmate back at Big Sur, I was a true adult now. Things would surely be different this time. Plus, if I found within the first 20 minutes that this guy is a no-go, I could easily take that last sip and say "Thank you so much for the cup of joe. Better be on my way," and slip out the door. A dinner is going to run you an hour to an hour and a half, minimum.

So, we settled on a day and time, and we met at the designated spot. As per usual, Sophie helped me prepare, and I was dressed in casual blue jeans and a trendy, tight-fitting t-shirt. I got there a few minutes early, as I wanted to be the one watching him walk in, awkwardly, looking for me (as opposed to the other way around). I also wanted to ensure that I was able to snag a small table. The last thing I wanted to do was to have our first conversation held standing up, bobbling our drinks, dodging the take-out patrons.

As luck would have it, I arrived in plenty of time to grab a table and watch the door. I didn't have to wait too long, however, because he arrived a few minutes early as well. I recognized him instantly. Miraculously, he looked just like his profile picture. I had heard plenty of horror stories from other friends who dabbled in the online dating scene.

"Just wait," they would say. "You think you're about to meet up with Brad Pitt, but then in strolls Leatherface."

And, certainly, there is all manner of folly that can befall you in the online dating world. One of my girlfriends, Kristine, told me a particularly memorable online dating horror story that she endured the year prior. She said that she and some guy named Jason agreed to have a picnic for their first date, and they arranged to meet up at a local recreational area. She figured that was a safe and reasonable choice, as it was a popular park, so there would likely be plenty of people around. She warned me to never meet with someone for the first time in a desolated area. Creepy though it may seem, that was probably very sound advice.

She also liked the idea of a picnic; it seemed to her to be a low-cost, high-interaction date. "Why should we go to noisy bars or bustling restaurants when we are trying to get to know someone," she said. "A picnic is the perfect blend of casual and romantic, and it is peaceful enough that you can actually talk and connect." Her logic was sound; I couldn't disagree.

Kristine detailed the date clearly. She said she remembered walking from the parking lot, a bottle of wine and two glasses in tow, toward the man in question. She basically recognized him from his photograph, and he was sitting on a blanket with a picnic basket next to him. *Bingo! That's him,* she reasoned. His back was facing her, so she couldn't see his face completely, but she was pretty sure she had the right person. As she approached, she could tell he was doing something with his hands, but she couldn't tell what exactly. He was sort of hunched over, and his right arm was moving slowly. She remembers instantly fearing that he was performing the unthinkable. *Was he masturbating in public?* she thought to herself. As she drew closer, she tried to get that idea out of her mind, admonishing herself for even thinking such a crude and despicable thought. *Surely, he wouldn't be doing that. Right?* As she came up on him, she was simultaneously relieved and horrified to see that he was not actually masturbating on the blanket. Instead, he was sitting on the picnic blanket, next to the basket of food… barefoot, clipping his toenails.

"Honestly, Annabelle," she said with exasperation, "I am not sure which is worse!"

Apparently, the date was over before it began. Just as their eyes met, she quickly blurted out "Oh! Hi! I am so sorry. I was supposed to have a picnic date with you, but I think I left my dog inside the house. I need to run home and let him out." She then whipped around and race-walked to her car, never to speak to him again.

I laughed. "But you don't even have a dog."

"Whatever! He didn't know that. I just needed to get the hell out of dodge. There is no way I could eat a picnic lunch while I stared at his toenail trimmings."

We both erupted into laughter.

So, when I saw Francis enter the Starbucks, wearing a very respectable jeans and a casual button-down shirt, complete with clean, closed-toe shoes, I instantly felt relief flow through my veins.

***

The coffee date, itself, is a bit of a blur. I do remember thinking that he smelled nice and that he was charming. I think we talked about college and how weird it was to suddenly be adulting. I remember feeling butterflies in my stomach when, coffee long gone, he asked me if he could take me on a proper date later that week. "Sure," I said. "That would be nice."

Inside, I worried that he would not call when he said he would. Would this be Chip 2.0? I decided to push that unpleasant thought out of my mind and remain hopeful.

To my surprise, he called me the very next day, and we set up plans for our first *real* date. He told me that he couldn't stop thinking about me and said that he just couldn't wait to call. He then asked me if I enjoyed the beach. I thought *Yes! But please… no picnic!*

I told him that I did enjoy the beach, and he asked if I would like to rent beach cruisers and ride along the bike path. I was super enthusiastic about that idea, and I immediately agreed. It was a date.

As soon as I hung up, I ran into Sophie's room. "He called. He wants to take me to the beach to ride bikes. He said he couldn't stop thinking about me! I think he likes me!" I was talking a mile a minute.

"All right, all right. I'm so very glad to hear it. It's about time someone sees what a fine ass catch you are." She always knew just what to say to pump me up.

I told her the date was set for Saturday, and she joined me in my feverish anticipation. She helped me pick out the perfect "beach bike riding" outfit, and she talked me down when I started to doubt and second-guess his alleged affection for me. When Saturday finally came, and I was about to step out of the apartment, ready to embark on my first *real* date with Francis, Sophie whispered into my ear, "You are amazing. Make him earn you, Ann." I knew what she meant, and I appreciated her assurance.

Fortunately, the date was idyllic. We rode bikes, stopped for lunch at a cute little beach front café, and spent the evening sitting on the sand, watching the sun go down over the Pacific. I remember we talked about everything under that sun. We talked about where we came from and where we are going. We pondered, aloud, about the mysteries of life, and we agreed that pie was definitely superior to cake. We seemed to have so much in common.

We found ourselves regularly proclaiming "Me too!" when one of us revealed a specific and seemingly obscure fact about our lives. We enjoyed the same pastimes, and we seemed to have similar goals for our future. I couldn't help it; I was feeling particularly hopeful about this one.

If our first date was ideal, our second date was close to perfect. We caught the morning train south to San Diego and spent the afternoon walking through the beautiful seaside town. We ate an early dinner at my favorite Mexican restaurant in the city, and we watched a live 80s cover band perform at a quaint bar on the beach. We sang along to all of our favorite songs, stopping only for a moment or two between sets to catch our breath. The train ride home was spent talking, laughing, and sharing comical anecdotes of our (mis)adventures thus far in the online dating scene. I told him about my one-and-done encounter with Marcus, and he threw his head back and shrieked, "Damn, Annabelle. You are savage."

He told me about a few of his lackluster dates, and I found myself feeling surprisingly jealous of these other women who got to spend time with him before me. This jealousy was quickly replaced with gratitude, however, as I realized that their loss was my gain. I felt incredibly excited and hopeful about our budding relationship.

Predictably, Mom was excited as well. "Oh, Annabelle, he is just terrific." It didn't hurt that he was employed in his lucrative family business (they owned a brand-new chain of doggie daycares in our area), and that he shared her love of animals, particularly canines.

Despite my kneejerk reaction to disagree with her, I really couldn't. I thought he was pretty terrific too.

Francis and I became inseparable over the next several months. We saw each other a handful of times during the week and almost every weekend. Conversation was easy with Francis, and we rarely, if ever, argued. We arranged romantic, overnight outings and talked, albeit vaguely, about the future. Our future. *Together*. Even Sophie thought he might be *the one*.

"You two are adorable together, Ann," Sophie said. "And as long as he treats you well, I'm happy. You deserve nothing but the best."

One particularly memorable outing with Francis was a day-long excursion to the Happiest Place on Earth. Growing up in Southern California, I had been to Disneyland more times than I could possibly count. However, having moved to Southern California somewhat recently from the Midwest, Francis had only been to Disney World in Florida, one time, as a young kid. He had never been to the OG in Anaheim.

I was excited to show Francis around the park. I became an expert tour guide, taking him on all the best rides (Space Mountain was his favorite), showing him the best places to eat (the churro cart near the castle for a snack… Café Orleans for lunch… Blue Bayou for a fancy dinner), and the best bathrooms to frequent (next door to Health Services in between Town Square and Tomorrowland, or next to Country Bear Jamboree if you're on the other side of the park). He was impressed with my random Disney trivia knowledge, and I was proud to show him around a place I had known so well since childhood.

We both enjoyed our time running around the amusement park like kids. We spun around in circles on the Mad-Hatter Teacups (Mad Tea Party), and we sang along to "Yo ho, yo ho, a pirate's life for me" on the Pirates of the Caribbean ride. He held my hand and snuck a quick kiss during the slow, dark rides like Snow White's Scary Adventures and the Haunted Mansion. He even bought me one of those obnoxious, ridiculously oversized Mickey Mouse ears balloons, as he remembered me mentioning that I used to beg my dad to buy me one as a child. Dad would always roll his eyes and say, "Come on, Annie. What are you going to do with a massive Mickey Mouse balloon?" Well, on this day, I was on cloud nine, walking through the park, gigantic balloon in one hand, Francis' hand in the other.

As the day fell into night, we made our way to back to Town Square. We staked out a prime spot to watch the Main Street Electrical Parade make its way from It's a Small World, through the heart of the park, and finally down along Main Street, U.S.A. We marveled at the thousands of twinkling lights and festive costumes. Just as the iconic Pete's Dragon float came into view, Francis leaned his head into mine and told me that he loved me. A warm feeling rushed throughout my entire body, and I reciprocated his sentiment. "I love you too, Fran" I whispered. Things were finally falling into place, and I felt great hope and optimism about our future.

My mother couldn't have been happier when I told her the news. I sighed. "He loves me, Mom,"

"Well of course he does, dear," she replied. "You are a darling woman, and he knows what a loving and devoted wife you will become."

As much as I wanted to roll my eyes and tell her that she is getting way ahead of herself once again and that we are taking it day by day and not to get her hopes up, I didn't. I couldn't. My hopes were up, and I did not want them to come down.

Unfortunately, all of this hopefulness I had possessed came to a screeching halt one crisp spring morning when I received an unthinkable phone call.

"Annabelle," the emotionless, robotic-sounding caller said, "this is Officer Smith. I regret to inform you that your parents have been in a serious automobile accident. They are enroute to the county hospital. You should come right away. It doesn't look good."

Chapter 13: Anguish

Isn't it weird how some memories come back to mind like crisp, vibrant recollections, and others are vague at best... disjointed images all fuzzy and blurred around the edges? It doesn't even necessarily matter how long ago the event in question took place. You could've asked me what I ate for dinner the night before, and I likely would have struggled to answer you. Other memories are different. They stay with you indefinitely. Some memories leave indelible marks on our psyches. What's more, the details of some events can't be erased no matter how hard we try. The events of this particular spring morning, April 6, was one of those days.

It was a Monday. I have always found it fitting that the worst thing that had ever happened to me (yes, even worse than Jefferson... even worse than Nash!), happened on a Monday. Mondays are simply the worst. There's no debate. Mondays are dumpster fires.

I remember that phone call as if it happened just mere moments ago. It was 8:04 a.m. when I answered it. I remember looking at the little digital clock that sat next to my bed just as the phone began to ring. I instantly felt a sense of dread wash over me the moment I heard it. The phone seemed to shriek in an ominous tone. How can that be? How would my body know to go cold with fear just from hearing the simple, prosaic sound of the telephone ringing?

With my hands trembling ever so slightly, I reached for the phone and hoped for the best. It was probably just a harmless telemarketer or an accidental wrong number. Who would be calling me at 8:04 am on a Monday morning anyway? Unfortunately, the best was not in store. The robotic-sounding police officer was on the other end of the line. He told me that my parents, who were on their way to my mother's annual dental checkup in their brand-new, midsized sedan, were hit head on by an SUV whose driver crossed the double yellow lines after he reportedly glanced away for "just a second" to change the radio station. One simple mistake, one brief lapse in focus, and my parents were now in an ambulance, racing toward the hospital, precariously clinging to life.

I wondered what had gone through my parents' minds as they saw that SUV swerve into their lane and approach them directly. Was it one of those moments that happens in slow motion? Did they see the absent-minded driver, looking down toward the car's console, and brace for certain impact? Or, did it all happen virtually instantly, in the blink of an eye? Was it like one moment they were just driving along, engaged in casual conversation, or listening to the news on their favorite AM talk radio station, and the next moment they were spinning around in circles before violently crashing into the center divider? I will probably never know the answer to that question, but I like to think it happened quickly and without too much dread, fear, or panicked anticipation. Yes, quick would have been so much better.

As I listened to the police officer deliver this dreadful and unbelievable news, time seemed to stand still for a few moments. It was like everything on earth stopped while he spoke. I could feel and hear my heart pounding inside my body, and I felt like I might collapse. I listened and nodded but was unable to verbally reply. I wanted to ask him questions. I wanted to know more details. However, I was rendered virtually mute. At the conclusion of his monologue, I swallowed hard and grunted "okay" into the receiver. It was all I could do to not vomit.

Almost on instinct, upon setting down the telephone receiver, I immediately picked that phone back up and quickly dialed Francis. I was surprised that I was able to dial it properly on the first attempt, as I was shaking fairly steadily by this point. He answered on the third or fourth ring. I was praying it would not go to voicemail. I really needed him right now. I remember saying something to the effect of "Oh my God, Francis. My parents were in a terrible car crash. I have to go to the hospital." I could barely choke out those vile and unbelievable words.

"Oh my God, Annie. That is awful. Are they okay?" He seemed genuinely shaken.

"I don't know. The police officer said it didn't look good. I'm scared, Francis." I was violently shaking by this point.

"Oh, shit, Ann. I am so sorry…" There was a long pause, and then he continued, "Damn. Let me know what happens, okay?"

It took me a couple of seconds to process what he just said. I suddenly felt a strong but fleeting burst of energy when he replied. Did I just hear him say what I think he said? "What do you mean 'let you know?' Aren't you coming with me?" I was sure I must have misunderstood.

"Oh, Annie. You know how I feel about hospitals…" his voice trailed off.

Do I? I thought, as I racked my brain…. *Do I know how he feels about hospitals?* I found myself racing through our many conversations, trying to recall if we ever had a discussion wherein we exposed our deep, innermost feelings about hospitals. I wasn't able to pinpoint anything.

"What? I mean, nobody likes hospitals, Fran" I said slowly, still searching my mind for the receipt of this alleged hospital conversation, trying desperately to remain erect and lucid.

"Yeah, but I like *really* hate hospitals, Annabelle. They freak me out. I just, you know, get a bad vibe in them. There's just no way I can go." He was almost impertinent, now, in this declaration.

Was this really happening? Was Francis just *not* going to go with me? Was he going to let me find my own way there and face this uncertain and terrifying fate all alone?

After an awkwardly long pause, he repeated, "Sorry, Babe. I just can't do it. I am sure your parents are fine, though. Cops always like to make things seem worse than they are. That's why they get into the criminal justice field in the first place. They love the drama." He seemed so sure of this verdict and so resolute in his decision to let me go it alone.

Briefly considering the absurdity of his statement, I replied, "Well, I sure as hell hope so," and I hung up the phone. I accepted the fact that Francis wasn't going to be there for me in my time of need. My heart sank, but I regained a bit of control, and I knew what I had to do. Turns out, this was the next to the last conversation I ever had with Francis.

***

Still in shock from Francis' cold refusal to accompany me, I did what I should have done from the very beginning. I called Sophie.

Just stepping into the law office to start her day, Sophie picked up my call on the first ring and, in a chipper, upbeat voice that rang out sweetly, she said: "You've got Sophie!"

By this point, I was already breaking down. I could hardly gather the strength to tell her the news, as uncontrollable sobs were coming now, in steady and persistent waves. "Parents... Crash... Hospital... Help…" is all I could muster to utter.

Without hesitation, she replied, "Oh my God! I will be right there. Just sit tight, Ann. Please don't worry. I will be there in just a minute."

I set the phone down. I am not even sure if I hung up the receiver. I just dropped it, and then I felt myself drop as well. As I was going down, knees buckling and head swaying as if it were a bowling ball on a pinpoint, I heard the strangest noise. It was primal. And penetrating. It was a guttural sound… almost like a moan and a howl… coming from somewhere close but also far away… somewhere nondescript. Little did I know that it was coming from inside me. I collapsed on the floor and listened to that haunting sound come and go as I wept, in violent sobs. I could have been there on the floor for seconds or for days. Time unilaterally stood still and stopped existing.

The next thing I remember was Sophie throwing open the front door, rushing in, and sweeping me into her arms. I buried my face in her hair and sobbed. "I'm scared, Soph! I am so, so scared!"

After that, my memory jumps to sitting in a chair in a stale and nearly empty room. There was a fake ficus tree in a decorative pot next to the door, and there were framed pictures of meadows and forests on the otherwise stark, white walls. Sophie was sitting next to me. A man walked in and made his way towards us.

Who is this man? I wondered. *Is he a doctor?* I thought. *Yes, he might be a doctor. He is wearing a long, white coat. Isn't that what doctors wear?*

Suddenly, I felt very confused. I didn't even remember the drive over to the hospital. My mind started racing and I began considering dozens of haphazard and disjointed thoughts. *Did I sit in the front seat of Sophie's car on our way here? Or, did we take my car? Was there any traffic? Did we speak to one another, or did we sit in silence? Did I remember to lock the front door of our apartment? Why is it so cold in here? Where am I again? How did we make our way into this empty room? What am I wearing? We must have gone through some sort of front desk or reception area when we arrived, right? Did we do that? Did I sign a piece of paper? Did we speak to anyone?* The last thing I clearly remembered was Sophie bursting through the front door of our apartment and sweeping me into her arms as I bawled my eyes out.

When was that? I tried to recollect. *Was that today?*

This man in the long, white coat interrupted my musings and asked if he could sit with me. I heard someone say yes.

Who said that? Was it Sophie? Was it me?

"Annabelle, I have some painful news…" the man in the long, white coat said. After a moment or two, he continued, "They didn't make it. I am so very sorry. There was nothing we could do."

Nothing that the long, white coat man said was making any sense.

"Who didn't make it?" I questioned.

He took a deep breath and continued, "Your parents, Annabelle. Your father was gone upon arrival, and your mother went within the hour. The injuries they sustained were extensive. Their bodies could not survive the trauma. Unfortunately, they simply gave out. I am so sorry." The long, white coat man seemed genuinely disappointed to deliver this news.

I looked up at Sophie, still in a daze. "What is he saying, Soph?"

"Oh, Annie. It's your parents, honey. They didn't make it." She swallowed hard and continued a moment later. She realized I needed some hard truths to penetrate my obvious shock. "They passed away, Ann" she said, as she visibly held back tears of her own. "They're gone."

I opened my mouth to speak, but nothing came out. I suddenly felt very light. I looked down at my body, and I could have sworn that it was translucent, almost see-through. As I examined my hands and marveled at my uncanny appearance, I started to feel something unusual. Slowly, I felt myself rising up. *Am I beginning to stand?* Up, up, up I went. I watched the bright white ceiling of this room, lined with florescent lights, get closer and closer. I glanced down, and I saw the most bizarre and unsettling sight. There was a man, he looked to be a doctor, talking to two women who were seated in chairs across from him. One woman had her eyes closed and was shaking her head back and forth, and the other woman was holding the other's hand repeating the phrase "It's okay, Annie. I promise. It will be okay."

Is there another Annie? I thought. *Wait. Isn't that Sophie? To whom is she speaking?*

"Come back to me, Annie. Come back," Sophie repeated.

With that, it was as though Sophie reached her hand up and grabbed ahold of me as I floated closer to the ceiling, about to be lost into oblivion. She seized hold of my hand and it felt as though she forcibly pulled me back down to the ground, back into my body. I was no longer transparent, nor was I feeling weightless. Instead, I felt incredibly heavy, and my head pounded. I took a deep breath and opened my eyes. Staring back at me was my best friend, tears in her eyes, and love in her voice, promising me that it was going to be ok.

I wanted to believe her, but how could it be okay? How would anything ever be okay again? Nothing made sense. How could my parents be gone? This must be a cruel joke… a terrible misunderstanding. Certainly, someone would wake me from this nightmare, and I would feel relieved to discover it was all just a bad dream. But nobody woke me up. Nobody admitted to pulling this malicious prank. As the dreadful reality settled upon me, I felt as though my body was suddenly an empty shell. I was gone too, it seemed. Everyone was gone, and what was the point of any of it, anyway? It was a dark and desperate time for me. Fortunately, one person wasn't gone: Sophie. Sophie was right there with me through all of it. Sophie was always my constant.

By some miracle, Sophie helped me to stand up, and she and I walked slowly toward the door. She grabbed me by the hand and tenderly led me out of the hospital, through the parking lot, and into her car.

Oh. I thought. *We did take Sophie's car.*

Sophie told me we would deal with any formalities and paperwork later. For now, she wanted to get me home and let me rest. I didn't have the wherewithal to protest. I could barely even form a cogent thought. Looking back on it days later, I realized I should have asked to see them. This is something I have always regretted. Why didn't I ask to see my parents and to say goodbye one last time? Did they know that I loved them? Did they know that I was proud to be their daughter? Did they know that, despite our occasional quarrels, they meant the world to me? Did they know that I would miss them, every day, with every fiber of my being, for the rest of my life? I hope they knew. I like to believe they did.

Although I eventually made it through these dark days, this tragedy became the defining moment in my life thus far. There were two distinct people who lived inside of me after this calamity. There was Annie BC (before crash) and Annie AD (after death). They were two completely different people sharing one body, mind, and soul.

Annie BC thought her parents were quite annoying sometimes. Annie AD realized that she would take annoying over vanished any day.

Annie BC thought she knew heartbreak. Annie AD laughed at that foolish notion.

Annie BC thought her greatest life struggle would be to find her Prince Charming. Annie AD understood that her greatest life struggle was going to be learning to live a life without her parents in it.

Thankfully, Annie BC and Annie AD had one thing in common: they both had Sophie.

Chapter 14: Reverberations

What followed in the immediate aftermath of this catastrophe was a fog so dark and so dense that almost nothing could penetrate it. It was like the depression I suffered following my breakup with Marshall but multiplied by about a billion. My heart felt heavy, like it was being squeezed in an unforgiving vice in my chest. The pain was palpable and inescapable. I sincerely wondered if I would ever smile, laugh, or feel pleasure again. Hell, I wondered if I would ever feel *anything* except pain again. I couldn't focus. I couldn't sleep. I couldn't eat. I could barely breathe. I found myself feeling guilty if I enjoyed even the most basic of human functions. *How dare I enjoy an apple,* I would think to myself, *when Mom and Dad will never eat again?*

Nighttime was unbearable. I would toss and turn in my bed, unable to fall asleep, haunted by nightmares of their final moments. Yet, I was also incapable of getting up and doing anything else even halfway productive. I was trapped in a prison of insomnia, anxiety, and grief. During the day, I would find myself walking aimlessly through the apartment, not knowing why I was walking, where I was going, or what I was doing. I would find myself in the kitchen or the bedroom, holding a ballpoint pen and a spoon. *Where did these come from? What am I supposed to do now*? I would wonder. Sophie was becoming increasingly concerned. I know this because I overheard her telling her boss she would need to stay home for a little while. This was completely unlike her. She was a tremendously driven woman whose career was on the upswing. She had just made junior associate at her law firm, and she was committed to hustling and showing the name partners what she was made of. Although part of my brain knew that I should feel guilty for Sophie taking a leave of absence from work on account of me, the other part of my brain forgot to register it.

I remained in this stupor for what seemed like an eternity. According to Sophie, it really only lasted a few days. Although I managed to technically remain employed, I walked a precarious tightrope. I wasn't able to communicate with my bosses, but luckily Sophie handled all of that for me. Fortunately, she had visited me enough times at *Sunshine Grill* to know my new manager on a first-name basis, and she explained the dire circumstances in which I had presently found myself. Gratefully, my manager showed some humanity and wrote me off the schedule for a couple of weeks. Sophie also kept my side-hustle going and wrote all the apartment copy for me as well. Between her own job, tending to me, and writing copy for the apartment-finding website, Sophie was burning the candle at both ends. Thanks to Sophie, however, my employment ship stayed afloat.

Apparently, on Thursday of that first week, Francis called. I wasn't completely sure what day it was or how much time had elapsed since my parents died, but I knew it was fairly long. Too long. Sophie handed me the phone and put her hand over the receiver so the person on the other end could not hear her speak. "Francis is on the phone. Do you even want to talk to him?" she asked. I could sense the irritation in her voice. She clearly did not approve of this phone call or this caller.

I said, "Who?" I was still so confused about everything. I hardly remembered my own name let alone anyone else's. And besides, what was a phone used for, anyway?

Sophie just hung her head and told the caller I wasn't feeling well and to try calling back at another time. Then, she abruptly hung up.

By the weekend, I was starting to feel partially human. I still couldn't sleep much, and food had lost its appeal, but I was in a *slightly* better head space. At least I was tracking basic reality and could generally function unassisted. I still endured the intense pain of my heartbreak, but at least I could think more lucidly. Sophie remarked that she could tell I was feeling better because I remembered to flush the toilet after I had peed. I guess it was a low bar.

That Sunday, a full week after the crash, Francis called again. I was able to take the call this time and, despite Sophie's mild protest and severe eye rolling, she handed me the phone.

"Hey" I said. I didn't really know how to start this conversation. Part of me was upset that he had taken so long to reach out, but the other part of me gave him the benefit of the doubt. Didn't he call earlier in the week? I had a suspicion that he did, but everything was so blurry and hazy. I couldn't seem to remember clearly. He probably tried to call and stop by several times. Sophie probably kept him from me in order to help me get myself back together a bit first. At least, that's what I wanted to believe. It's what I told myself in that moment.

"Hey," he replied. "How are you?"

"Well, "I said with a long sigh, "I am not great. I mean, I'm alive. But, my parents aren't, so there's that...." I realize this was not an elegant way to let my boyfriend know that my parents had died, but I just sort of blurted it out.

"Yeah, I heard. Sorry, Annie," he replied.

"Yeah, me too."

Several seconds passed before either one of us spoke. I really wasn't sure what to say, so I guess I waited for him to make the next move.

"So, hey," he said finally. "Anyway, I am really sorry again about your parents and everything. Wow. What a blow. Unreal. That just sucks. It really does. God, it's just so unbelievable." He seemed to be beating around the bush a bit. I wondered where this conversation was going to go. He finally continued, "But listen, anyway, I just need to confirm that are we still on for seeing Dave Grohl's new band up North next weekend. I was thinking we could leave Thursday, late morning, to, you know, beat the traffic. We can take Interstate 5. It's a less picturesque view, but it is faster than heading up 395. We will save money on gas that way. I figure we can stay Thursday night in the Bay Area somewhere before heading on to Tahoe early Friday morning. There are plenty of places to stay in the city, and I am sure we can find something affordable. The concert is not until Saturday night, so we will want to be there the day before so we can explore Tahoe a bit Friday night and Saturday morning, and then be ready to pregame before the show Saturday night. If we arrive in Tahoe Friday afternoon, we should have plenty of time."

I was stunned. I did not know how to respond. Was he really talking about the Foo Fighters? Did he expect that I would be able to track all of these logistical details at this moment? Moreover, did he imagine I was mentally, physically, and spiritually prepared to take a road trip and see a concert just days after losing my entire family in one fell swoop?

After a couple of seconds, I responded: "What?"

"Dave Grohl. Foo Fighters. Annie, are you listening? We have so many details to firm up. Are we renting a car, or driving mine? I am not sure yours will hold up for that kind of distance. You already have more than 100,000 miles on yours. If we take mine, I will need to get an oil change first. That's why I am thinking we might just want to rent a car. I am sure we can get a modest compact car for a good deal. My dad's brother used to work for Hertz. He might be able to hook us up. I also need to make sure we get the hotel reservations, and I definitely need to stop and get some booze. You know how I hate paying $10 for well drinks at the concert venue. That's why we need to pregame before heading out on Saturday night. As you can see, there is a lot for me to do here. I really need your head in the game right now, Annie."

He spoke as if this were a normal conversation on a normal day with a normal person who hadn't just lost her whole family.

I was in stunned disbelief. I took a moment to collect my thoughts.

"Hello, Earth to Annie. Are you there?" he asked in half jest. "I'm waiting...!" there was a tone of irritation in his voice.

That last comment felt like a rusty knife penetrating my already frail chest and driving into my already shattered heart. *Is he for real?*

I finally spoke. "I'm sorry, Francis. Are you seriously asking me if we are still on to take a vacation when I was literally just orphaned a couple of days ago?" The tone of my voice definitely screamed *what the fuck, man!?*

He snorted and huffed, "Annie, don't turn this on me. This is not my fault. As you know, I had absolutely nothing to do with what happened. Yes, it is a terrible tragedy what happened to your parents. Yes, you suffered a loss. Yes, I wish it never happened. Frankly, I hope they fry that motherfucker who hit them." He stopped for a dramatic pause. Then, he continued, "But life goes on. Blowing off your boyfriend is not going to bring them back, Annie. And, might I remind you that we have had this trip idea planned for quite a while. Um, in case you don't remember, it's also my birthday weekend, Annie. My 30th birthday. My *Dirty Thirty*! I can't believe you are even balking at this. Please don't tell me that you have forgotten about my birthday."

He paused to allow me to reply. When I stayed silent, he continued his barrage: "Are you even serious right now? Are you messing with me? Wait. Am I on Candid Camera? This must be some sort of savage joke, right? You cannot be serious, Annabelle." I was stunned by his inappropriately aggressive and sarcastic tone.

Sadly, my initial knee-jerk reaction was to feel terribly guilty and bend over backwards to make him feel better. It was his 30th birthday after all. It wasn't his fault that my life was crumbling. He didn't kill my parents. Why should he suffer the consequences? *Am I out of line*, I wondered? *Am I a monster?* But then, seemingly out of nowhere, a sudden and fierce sobriety hit me, and I sat up straighter in my chair.

"Are you kidding ME, Francis? My parents just died. I am in mourning. I am *suffering*. You think you have details to tend to? Are you fucking kidding me? I also have plans to consider, Francis. I have many people to call, and I have many decisions to make, decisions that I never dreamt I would be put in the situation to even consider. I need to determine what to do with all of my parents' personal belongings. I need to decide if they should be buried or cremated. I need to figure out if I have access to their financial documents. For fuck's sake, Francis, I have to find a home for their two dogs and three cats! I cannot just casually walk away from this tragedy, forget that it happened, and go gallivanting off to Lake Tahoe to celebrate your precious birthday!" I was shell shocked and furious.

Abruptly, and without warning, all of the little red flags that I had ignored over the last several months came crashing into my brain. I suddenly recollected all of the times he gaslighted me into thinking I had made a mistake when I had been pretty sure I hadn't… or when I ignored the fact that he was being extremely selfish about an issue that was important to me, and I simply chalked it up to a miscommunication or even an unrealistic expectation on my part. Suddenly, these unpleasant memories came crisply into view. And besides that, how could he be, in this very moment, so entirely tone-deaf? Did he hear himself at all? Did he care that he was rubbing salt in my gaping wound? How could he turn my personal tragedy into an affront against him? I instantly realized that this idyllic relationship was only pretty on the outside. It was a measly shell of a relationship, clearly… utterly hollow and vapid on the inside. It was window-dressing, superficial costume jewelry at best.

Apparently, Francis remained unfazed by my heartfelt confession. "Wow, Annie. Just wow," he said with obvious surprise and contempt. "I can't believe you are doing this to me. You are being incredibly selfish. I mean, I am obviously very sorry that your parents died and whatever, but why are you doing this to me? Flaking out on me, on my birthday no less, is NOT going to bring them back. This is unbelievable. I am absolutely dumfounded right now, Annie." He spoke with shock and confusion in his voice. But beneath that shock there was also something else. I am pretty sure I detected actual disdain.

"Honestly, Annie," he continued, "I think I need to take some time to evaluate whether or not this relationship is even going to work. I am not sure I can be with someone who treats me like this."

I remained silent, unable to speak at this moment. My mind was processing this interaction, and I was literally rendered speechless.

Finally, after another long pause for dramatic flair, he added: "Frankly, Annie, I think I deserve better."

So, there it was. Francis couldn't believe I had the nerve to cancel plans with him because both of my parents, the only family I had left on the face of this planet, had the nerve to die right before his special birthday. This was the same man who refused to take me to the hospital during my most desperate time of need, because he didn't "like hospitals." So many disjointed thoughts and emotions started racing through my mind. Amid the chaos whirling around in my head, however, I suddenly had one cogent and profound realization: had he taken me to the hospital when I first asked him, I might have seen my mother still alive. I remembered something the long, white coat man had said to me in that stark, white room on that fateful day: "Your father was gone upon arrival, and your mother went within the hour."

I suddenly realized that I wasted valuable time calling Francis, pointlessly begging him to take me to the hospital, before doing the smart and sensible thing and calling Sophie. Although I will never know for sure, the mere thought that it could be true that he spoiled my chances of seeing my mother alive one last time ignited a rage in me so deep and so profound that I made an abrupt but resolute decision right then and there.

"Let me save you the trouble of thinking it over, Francis," I said between gritted teeth. "It's over. We are over. Done. Finished. End of story. Lose my number. Oh, and one more thing: Go fuck yourself!"

And THAT was my last conversation with Francis.

Chapter 15: Reckoning

I wish I could say that Francis was my last toad. I wish I could say that after sending Francis packing, my life just miraculously and effortlessly fell into place. I wish I could say that I met and fell in love with a handsome, charming, and noble prince who rescued me from my anguish and saved me from my grief. Sadly, that is not exactly the case. Frankly, it's not even *almost* the case.

The weight of adult life without my parents in it was a lot for me to bear, and I didn't handle it with as much grace as I could have. I was suddenly the oldest person in my family. Christ, I was the *only* person in my family. I had to learn to navigate the world with my GPS obliterated. Sure, I had Sophie to lean on, but she could only do so much. I was the final architect, after all, of my life. It was during this point in time that I really began to lament my college years. Would I ever again experience a time in my life as beautiful, easy, and full of promise? In college, Annie BC was on top of the world; she was living her best life, with her best friend, every single day. She had her parents there as her safety net and her ultimate support system. Back then, she was just one mere moment away from meeting her prince and living out her destiny. How did it all go so wrong?

Was my mother right? Did I squander the best years of my life? Did I succeed in earning my "BA" degree but fail in getting my "MRS?" One of the songs that both haunted and comforted me during this phase of my life was "These Are Days" by 10,000 Maniacs.

Something about the way Natalie Merchant honored this meaningful time in her life truly resonated with me and evoked a sense of nostalgia that was palpable. I remembered all the fun and carefree times I had in high school and college, at Big Sur, and with Sophie in our tiny, little on-campus apartment. How I longed to be back in that time of my life. It was a time when anything was possible. My parents were alive and well, and life was just beginning to make sense. I reproached myself for not appreciating these beautiful days more while I was living them. Isn't that one of the ironic hallmarks of being human? Why does life only seem to make sense in reverse? While these carefree days of endless possibility seemed to be in the distant past, somehow this song helped me to remain hopeful that better days could also be ahead, even though I lamented their passing. Even during my darkest hours, I was waiting for that *shaft of light to make its way across* my *face*. Maybe these days could and *would* return. Just maybe.

After unceremoniously saying farewell to Francis, I hopped into several more questionable and problematic relationships. After suffering through the grief and anguish of losing my parents, I found myself drowning my sorrows in tequila and messy relationships. Annie AD plummeted in a downward spiral for quite some time. Poor Sophie had to watch me and feel feckless to help. Regrettably, it took a while for me to turn that ship around.

To paint a picture of this descent, I dated one toad who was most likely a speed dealer. He had a regular job, but he seemed to have more energy and more money than he should have had with his alleged, average 9 - 5 office gig. He very clearly had some sort of shady, side hustle going on. He was always a little bit fidgety and sweaty, and he regularly held clandestine meetings with equally sketchy, jittery people in what could be considered seedy and unsavory locations. He met these random people in places like dark, desolate alleys or in run-down laundromats at the edge of town. I didn't usually accompany him on these outings, but I did have the misfortune of tagging along one or two times. When I did, he always insisted that I stay in the car (with the windows rolled up and doors locked, no less) while he ran out for a minute to "talk to a friend, really quick." This should have been a dead giveaway that something wasn't kosher. Of course, I never told Sophie about any of these red flags. She already didn't approve of him due to the fact that he refused to look her in the eye. She felt that he was clearly hiding something, and she didn't trust him one bit. Moreover, she was disgusted by the fact that he called me "Anniebelle."

"It's either Annabelle or Annie," she would argue. "'Anniebelle' just makes him sound stupid." She couldn't believe I wasted my time with him.

Further, Sophie did not care for the fact that he regularly showed up at our apartment well past midnight. "What the hell kind of job does he have anyway, Annie?" she would ask, under her breath, as she walked past us in the dark.

Sophie didn't trust him, and she couldn't understand what I saw in him. Truth is, I saw what I needed to see at that moment: someone, anyone, to distract me from the unbearable pain I was in.

One time, when I was stranded in his car while he ran one of his urgent errands, I became a little bored and started looking (okay, one might call it snooping) around in his car. I was startled and quite alarmed when I opened the glove box and found a pistol, tucked neatly behind a stack of McDonalds napkins. I didn't touch it, and I have no idea if it was loaded, but it certainly got my attention. Luckily, that gun scared me straight. I broke it off with him before anything too dire happened. Years later, I heard that he had been tragically killed in a drive-by shooting. Sophie says I may have dodged a bullet, literally.

Another toad I dated was religious zealot. At first, I thought this was a good thing. Perhaps he could save my ever-loving soul. I knew I was spiraling, and I thought I could possibly cling to him for safety and security. For the most part, he seemed like a decent guy. He was devoted to his church, and he treated me kindly and with respect.

After a couple of weeks of casual dating, he invited me to join him at a church service. I hadn't been to church since my parents dragged me to Sunday school every weekend as a child, so I wasn't entirely sure what to expect. The first red flag was that the service was not held in a building. Rather, there were folding chairs set up in the parking lot of an abandoned old warehouse. *It's fine,* I thought. *Church doesn't need to be in a chapel. God can find us anywhere.* As I was told in my youth, where two or more are gathered in His name, He is there. It didn't need to be a fancy or lavish temple, synagogue, tabernacle, mosque, or cathedral. It could be anything, anywhere. However, within a few minutes of the service, my intuition told me that something was off. Looking back, I think he was part of some sort of cult or something, because the next thing I knew, one of the parishioners went up and down the aisles asking for volunteers to try some mystery potion. He said it would "cure what ails you," but it was yellowish-green and smelled like formaldehyde and cigarette butts. *Nope, I don't think so.* I respectfully declined the unappetizing brew. My date was not at all happy that I turned it down, and he was sure to let me know later that I humiliated him in front of his pastor. I questioned aloud what one had to do to become a pastor of a parking lot parish, and let's just say that this particular line of questioning was also not appreciated. He let me know he would no longer be requiring the *pleasure* of my company. Touché, my man. The feeling was mutual.

The worst toad I dated during this troubled time was an absolute loser with a capital L. He was unemployed and, frankly, unemployable. He basically used me for anything and everything I had to offer… money, validation, a place to stay, sex… He treated me the way that I sadly felt I deserved to be treated at this point in my life: with disdain and derision. He would regularly ridicule me for any number of my personal qualities. I liked to read? I was a boring bookworm. I was gainfully employed? I was a puppet of the man. I made a point of recycling my aluminum cans? I was a radical, hippie, tree-hugger. It never crossed my mind at the time that he was terribly inconsistent in his indictment of me. Pick a lane, buddy. Was he a conservative douchebag or a liberal hack? I guess he was simply a self-interested degenerate. As it were, he continued to treat me with such unbelievable disrespect that Sophie finally squared up to him and told him (and this is verbatim) *he had better get the fuck out of my life or she would hunt him down and sever his dick from his crotch.* Unsurprisingly, he didn't stick around to call her bluff.

***

All of these bad decisions came to a head one evening a couple of weeks later. Sophie sat me down and decided to offer up some tough love. She let me know, in no uncertain terms, that I was royally fucking up my life and that she couldn't, moreover, that she *wouldn't,* watch me destroy myself or settle for some douchebag of a man.

I will remember that evening for the rest of my life. I was reclined on the couch in the living room. I had been there for several hours, listlessly watching infomercials, picking at some left-over pasta. I was numb all over, honestly. I knew I was flailing, but I couldn't seem to shake myself out of it.

Sophie walked in from work. I am sure she was exhausted, as she was regularly putting in 12-hour days back then. She came over to the couch, glanced down at me, and shook her head, disapprovingly. She grabbed the remote control, and she snapped off the TV.

"Hey!? What are you doing?" I asked rather despondently… more of a comment than a question. I neither cared that she turned off the television nor did I necessarily want to know why.

"I am worried about you, Ann." She said with sincere concern in her voice.

"I'm fine, Soph," I said in a robotic sounding voice.

Sophie asked if she could sit down. I moved my legs to make room and she saddled up next to me. She turned to face me, and she grabbed my hands in hers. She looked me dead in the eyes and she said, with a firmness in her voice that shook me at the time, "Annabelle. You cannot go on like this. I love you too much to watch you throw your life away with booze and abusive and meaningless relationships."

Part of me was startled. Sure, she had delivered hard news to me before, but something about the way she looked into my soul made me catch my breath. Another part of me was angry. How could she judge me in a time like this? Doesn't she know how devastated I am to have suffered this loss?

"Fine, Sophie," I said with a cold dismissal, "don't watch then." I tried to take my hands out of hers, but she tightened her grip. She kept her eyes fixed on mine. She wouldn't let me go.

"What are you doing?" I cried, a little shocked that she was doubling down on her death grip, but also a little intimidated by her resolution. I tried to sort of squirm away, but she wouldn't let me go.

"I told you, Ann," she repeated in that same stern yet somehow equally loving tone, "I love you too much to watch you throw your life away. Your parents are gone. I know how much that hurts. I know you feel like part of you died right then and there with them. I know that nothing makes any sense to you right now. But you are here, damn it. You are here, and you are alive, and I will not let you do this to yourself."

I interrupted her and yelled, "You're right! They are dead! Everything is fucked!" I couldn't believe she had the audacity to hassle me with a lecture when I was sitting there, orphaned and grieving. I thought my outburst would do the trick and she would leave me alone to wallow in peace.

However, my little tantrum simply made her more determined. "Yes, your parents are dead. But guess what,

Annabelle? You are not dead. You are alive, and you are here. I will not let you waste your life because you are confused or because you are in pain. Your parents wouldn't want that for you, and I don't want that for you." She squeezed my hands even tighter, not letting me writhe away. She pressed on, "You have absolutely everything to live for, and you mean absolutely everything to me. I won't let you go, Annabelle. I. WILL. NOT. LET. YOU. GO!"

I felt like her words were a dart penetrating my thin veneer and lodging directly into my heart. I could see tears forming in her eyes as she worked persistently to convey her message. I ultimately knew that she was right (shocker!) and that I was making a terrible mess of my life. My mind flashed back to every stupid decision I had made over the past year, and I felt instantly nauseated. I was filled with terrible regret and remorse. Without thought and without warning, I burst in tears. I was weeping in uncontrollable sobs. I was "ugly crying" (as she told me many years later). In desperation, I reached out to her, and I clutched her in a powerful embrace. I clung to her as I wept, repeating the words "I'm scared, Sophie. I'm falling, and I'm scared" over and over again.

She held me tighter as I wailed, and she kissed the top of my head. After what felt like an eternity, I finally began to calm down, and my violent cries turned to quiet whimpers. After some time, she finally released her tight embrace, and she took my hands in hers. After a moment, she let go. She smoothed back my hair that had fallen in front of my eyes, and she held my face in her hands. She directed my eyes to meet hers, and she repeated without blinking or stammering or stuttering: "I've got you, Annabelle. I've got you, and I will never let you go."

This is the moment I knew. This is the moment I had longed for, even before I knew it was possible to long for it. This was the inevitable moment that I could not escape, nor did I want to. This is the moment my questions were answered, and my confusing feelings were defined.

We looked into each other's eyes for many moments, neither one of us breaking our intense gaze. I felt something stirring inside of me that I had felt before but that I could never properly identify, define, or describe. My heart was pounding inside of my chest, and my pulse was racing. I finally broke the silence that laid thick between us, and I said, "I love you, Sophie. I have always loved you."

Her eyes grew wet, and I saw a tear fall silently down her cheek.

Without thinking, I wiped that tear from her beautiful face, and I reached my arms around her, bringing her close to me. I could feel her breathing start to quicken, and her hands began to tremble as she wrapped them around my waist. I closed my eyes, and I placed my quivering lips on hers. The moment they touched, I felt an electric pulse race throughout my body unlike anything I had ever felt before or since.

She gasped and said "Annie," with a breathless tension that seemed both surprised yet also excited. I slowly replied, "Yes, Sophie. Yes."

With that, I leaned my entire body into hers, and I kissed her deeply and passionately. I could feel her heart pounding beneath her shirt. It was pounding right alongside of mine. I slowly stood up, and I grabbed her hand. I helped her up, and I led her off the couch. I walked her to the bedroom, and I laid her tenderly on my bed. We slowly removed our clothes, not uttering a word but still knowing exactly what to do. Her hands explored every inch of my body, and my heart sang with delight. We made love to each other that evening with a passion and a veracity that was palpable. I had never experienced desire the way that I had enjoyed it that night. We both moaned with pleasure and in ecstasy, and all of the pain and heartbreak I had suffered suddenly vanished. We watched the sun peer into the room that next morning, as we clung to each other, still wrapped in our gentle embrace. We both fell silent, each wondering what the other was thinking, hoping that our thoughts were in synch, afraid to speak, lest we break the magic spell we were under… and wondering, above all, what now…?

Chapter 16: Postscript

That night with Sophie came to be the night that everything changed for me. True, it hadn't been the prettiest couple of years following my parents' death. I made some mistakes, that's for sure. Fortunately, no mistake was so enormous that I couldn't recover. I wasn't arrested for anything, I didn't kill anyone, and, by some miracle, I did not contract an STD. If I really consider the possibilities, it could have been so much worse. And, fortunately, through it all, Sophie was there by my side, propping me up when I couldn't stand on my own, and reminding me that life may not be perfect, but it is precious. And fortunately, after a handful of years, and countless hours of therapy, I finally figured it out and I settled into adulthood. *Real* adulthood. Adulthood where I no longer needed anyone else's approval. Adulthood where I knew my worth. Adulthood where I made peace with the fact that who I was and who I wanted to be could actually become the same person. Yes, Annie AD has survived. Nay, she has thrived.

And of course, I know there is still the burning question of my love life. Fortunately, I am happy to report, I did find my one true love. We have made a tender and fulfilling life together with three beautiful children, a loving home, and, of course, a faithful pup. It has been an incredible adventure. Sure, there have been some challenges, but there have been far more "ups" than "downs." Honestly, it has been so much more than I ever expected… even more than I could have dared to dream.

And, here I sit now, more than 20 years later, recollecting my life and my many mishaps and successes. That's what life is, right? A series of average events, punctuated by moments of great sorrow and sometimes of great elation. And really, isn't it strange how quickly life flies by? I remember when I was a kid, I would hear adults saying things like that and I would think to myself *Ok, that is just stupid. Are you demented? Life flies by? That's a boldfaced lie. Life goes by at a snail's pace! Wait for Christmas? It's 8 months away! 8 months is a lifetime!* But now, with the wisdom of maturity, I clearly see what they were talking about. I blinked, and now my life is half over (if I'm lucky).

I often wonder if my mom can see me from wherever she is. If she can, would she be happy? Would she be proud? Despite our occasional quarrels, I believe she sincerely loved me and did just want the best for me. She wanted me to be happy… to be fulfilled. To her, happiness may have been defined by satisfying social norms and complying with the expectations of our society. From her perspective, that meant being a wife and a mother. Predictably, she wanted the same thing for her only daughter. Sometimes, I talk to her when I am feeling nostalgic or when I am feeling lost. I get weepy thinking about the sacrifices she made in her own life and wonder if, all things considered, she would do it again. She grew up in the 1950s and 60s, and at that time, she felt that there was no greater position in life for a woman than to be a homemaker. Would she feel that way in 2024? What's more, did she *truly* feel that way then?

Ultimately, I think she would be happy and proud if she could see me now. The irony is, despite our occasional disagreements and my conscious rebellion against all things domestic, I actually did become a wife and mother after all. Go figure. And, hey, and I finally found out what you can do with an English major: you can write a book! Ta-da.

Most notably, I finally kissed enough toads that I was able to find my *one true love*. The only catch? I didn't actually find my prince. I found something much better: I found my princess.

On my birthday in 2004, 20 years ago now, Sophie and I made our way up North to San Francisco and obtained our official marriage license. We had a beautiful ceremony in our Southern California hometown a few weeks later, surrounded by her large, boisterous, and loving family and all our loyal and faithful friends. It was an incredible event that could only have been made better had my parents been there to participate. People have asked me if I think they would have been supportive of our marriage. Although I suppose I will never know for certain, I can only imagine that they would have been. They loved Sophie, and they loved me. Isn't that all we really need in this world? In the end, I think they simply and exclusively wanted me to be happy. And, happy, I most definitely am.

Despite the fact that we are now, all these years later, an "old married couple," our love story was not necessarily simple, nor was it a straight line. I realize it probably began (unbeknownst to us at the time) back when we first laid eyes on each other in high school. We just didn't know how to interpret those weird feelings we felt in the pit of our stomachs when we were together. Butterflies, perhaps, but also something deeper, heavier, and more robust. But, like most meaningful things in life... it was complicated. Regrettably, at that time, society told us that loving each other was forbidden and unthinkable. It's incredibly sad because loving one another is truly the most beautiful and important thing we can do as human beings. And loving Sophie has been the greatest joy and honor of my life. Fortunately, we were finally able to put a name to those feelings that beautiful night in our apartment when we threw caution to the wind, and we reveled in the love we had for one another. And, despite the predictable and unpredictable bumps we have faced through our life's journey together, we have promised to love each other—with body, mind, and soul—for the rest of eternity.

We have done that, and we continue to do that. Every. Single. Day.

Made in the USA
Middletown, DE
05 February 2025